GLADIATOR SCHOOL

BOOK 1

BLOOD OATH

DAN SCOTT

SCRIBO

A division of Book House

First published in Great Britain by Scribo MMXIII
Scribo, a division of Book House, an imprint of
The Salariya Book Company
25 Marlborough Place, Brighton, BN1 1UB
www.salariya.com

ISBN 978-1-908177-48-3

The right of Dan Scott to be identified as the author of this work has been asserted
in accordance with sections 77 and 78 of the Copyright, Designs
and Patents Act, 1988.

Book Design by David Salariya

Special thanks to Rachel Moss

© The Salariya Book Company
MMXIII

Printed and bound in India.
Reprinted in MMXV.

The text for this book is set in Cochin
The display type is P22 Durer Caps

www.scribobooks.com

GLADIATOR SCHOOL
BOOK 1

BLOOD OATH

DAN SCOTT

SCRIBO

A division of Book House

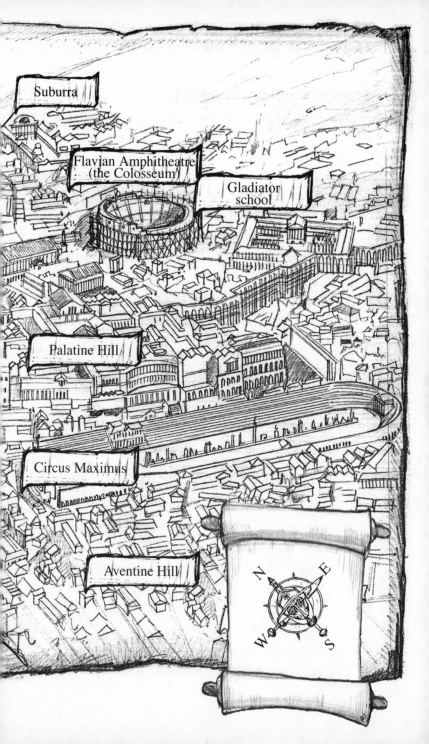

Introducing Gladiator School, a series of novels set in a rich and textured world of dusty arenas, heated battles, fierce loyalty and fiercer rivalry. Follow young Lucius as his privileged life is suddenly turned upside down, leading him to seek answers amongst the slaves and warriors who work and train at Rome's gladiator school.

What the lovereading4kids reader reviews say about *Blood Oath*:

'There is only one single bad thing about this book and that is that it ends!'
ADAM GRAHAM, AGE 9

'The beginning of this book really gripped me so I would not put it down.'
GRACE PARKER, AGE 10

'The gladiators fights were really exciting and sometimes I wasn't sure if they would live or die. If you like adventures with a touch of mystery you will love this book.'
SAM HARPER, AGE 9

'I enjoyed this book because I was sitting on the edge of my seat wondering what was going to happen next.'
SHAKRIST MASUPHAN-BOODLE, AGE 10

ROME
JULY AD 79

The Roman Empire flourishes; the world is at its feet and there is a new emperor in command. Determined to be a fair ruler, Titus has decided to put an end to trials and executions based on the hated Law of Treason. He plans to rid the Senate* of the networks of informers that have built up over the years.

Around the Senate, those who have informed on others dread discovery, and none more so than the most feared informer of all – the so-called Spectre.

When his real name is revealed, his freedom will be forfeit, and his family will suffer the shame and ignominy of his actions...

* Senate: the ruling council of ancient Rome.

THE MAIN CHARACTERS

Lucius, a Roman boy

Quintus, his older brother

Aquila, their father

Ravilla, their uncle

Caecilia, their mother

Valeria, their sister

Isidora, Lucius's friend, a slave

Rufus, a slave

Crassus, a trainer of gladiators

TRAITOR!

**ROME
JULY AD 79**

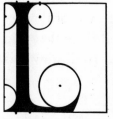 ucius stared at the household gods.

Everyone else seemed able to shout and cry and wail and rage, but Lucius couldn't even open his mouth. From the moment the soldiers had burst in to arrest his father and found him missing, Lucius's eyes had been glued to the little wooden statues.

The soldiers had stormed through the villa, overturning furniture, rattling their swords and yelling, 'We arrest you, Quintus Valerius Aquila; in the name of the Emperor, show yourself!'

His mother had collapsed, trembling, onto the couch in the atrium,* clasping Lucius's sister Valeria

---

* *atrium: the entrance hall of a Roman villa.*

close to her. Valeria, who was made of sterner stuff, had wriggled free and stared at the soldiers in round-eyed wonder.

Lucius's older brother had found plenty to say. Quintus, named after his father, was never lost for words. He had followed the soldiers through the villa as they searched for his father, warning them of the dire punishments that would fall on their heads when his father returned, threatening them with curses and finally invoking the household gods to protect the family against the intruders.

But, throughout it all, Lucius had stayed in the atrium, his back pressed against the cool marble walls. The statues were still wearing their crowns of flowers and leaves. Less than a day had passed since they had celebrated their mother's birthday. And now his world was crumbling around his ears.

'Where is he, boy?'

A soldier was standing in front of him, demanding an answer.

'The Senate?' snapped Quintus from the doorway to the atrium. 'The Forum?* Where else would you expect one of Rome's most respected senators to be at this time of day?'

'He's not there,' Lucius said.

His voice sounded croaky and unfamiliar.

'What are you talking about?' asked Quin.

---

* Forum: the marketplace of ancient Rome, which was also the place for business meetings and political discussions.

He sounded irritable and indignant. *How funny,* thought Lucius. *Quin always knows everything. How come he doesn't know this?*

'Explain yourself,' rapped out the soldier, who was evidently losing patience fast.

'Look,' said Lucius.

Finally, Quin followed the direction of his brother's gaze and his eyes fell on the altar. Lucius saw Quin's posture change. His shoulders sagged, his face registered confusion and disbelief.

'The dog's gone,' he said.

Of the three statues that represented their household gods, the wooden dog had always been their father's favourite. It had stood on the hearth altar for as long as Lucius could remember. Aquila had said that it represented the faithfulness of true friends. He would never take the statue on a normal working day. But it would always travel with him when he made a journey.

'He's taken the statue?' demanded the soldier.

Lucius nodded.

The soldier's mouth set into a grim line. 'Right,' he said.

He called his men and ordered them to his side.

'You're going?' Quin asked.

'Yes,' said the soldier. 'We'll leave you to your shame.'

'What's that supposed to mean?' Quin had recovered from his initial shock and was truculent again.

The soldier turned to stare at him. To this man, they were simply a job. He had no feelings about them, good or bad.

'It means that your father is a liar and an informer,' he said. 'It means that he's been found out and he's fled before he can be tried.'

Lucius looked away from the statues at last. Quin had gone very pale, and he was trembling.

'My father's not a traitor!' he declared.

But his words sounded empty, and the soldier clearly wasn't interested in what he had to say. Lucius's eyes fell on the hearth altar again. Whether their father was innocent or guilty, for some reason he had certainly left Rome. For now, they were on their own.

PART ONE

NOVICIUS

CHAPTER I

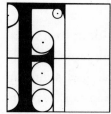'*ight!*' bellowed Crassus. 'This isn't *fighting*! Are you a baby? Are you a coward? FIGHT!'

The trainer grabbed Quin's arm, held it high in the air and punched him in the stomach. As Quin doubled forward in pain, Crassus jabbed him in the back with his elbow and then twisted him head over heels to the floor with a body-cracking thud.

'Show a little style!' Crassus yelled. 'Get up! Make it exciting!'

Lucius, watching his brother from the side, felt his stomach heave. He had felt the thud as Quin hit the sandy floor. It was only Quin's second day as a novicius* in the gladiator school. There would be many weeks – perhaps months – of this ahead of him.

Quin had always seemed strong and powerful. But now, standing barefoot in the middle of the arena, wearing nothing but a loincloth, he looked like a child. Blood and sweat were smeared across his back and shoulders.

Other novicii gladiators were watching from the side steps, and Lucius had ventured out of the back rooms of the school to see how Quin was getting on. Now he wished that he hadn't bothered.

'No sword, no shield, no armour,' he muttered. 'It's not fair.'

'They have to learn to fight with no kit at first,' said a voice behind him. 'The weapons come later.'

Lucius spun around and saw a slave girl standing there. Her thick, black hair hung in two heavy plaits around her oval face. Lucius didn't know what to say. A month ago he would have smiled and thanked her. He would have known his own status. Now, working in the gladiator school, he didn't even feel like himself any more. He certainly didn't feel like talking. He turned back to the arena, where Quin was on his back again.

One of the watching gladiators turned to Lucius. His lips parted in a black-toothed grin.

---

* *novicius (plural: novicii): a trainee gladiator.*

18

'Your brother's not even out of his swaddling clothes,' he said, spitting onto the sand. 'We eat his sort for breakfast.'

Clearly this gladiator was already trained and fighting for money. Lucius didn't answer but, as he heard another cry of pain from Quin, his throat burned. He would be sick if he kept on watching. He had to get out. Luckily, he had an excuse to leave: his uncle had asked him to deliver a message to someone in the Forum.

The sweltering streets of Rome seemed less busy than usual. Lucius wove his way towards the Forum, the cries of street sellers ringing in his ears as he darted through the throng of carts and chariots. The acid smell of urine and excrement stung his throat. He stumbled over a litter of piglets trotting across his path and the owner yelled at him: 'Out of the way, boy!'

'Sorry,' Lucius murmured, scooting to the side of the street, where a meat vendor who was selling piles of fresh red lungs was splattering everyone in the vicinity with blood.

He hadn't been paying too much attention to his route up till now. He knew the streets so well that his feet would carry him to the marketplace while his mind was still in the arena with his brother. But now he realised that he was standing on the street where their old home was. The shops set into the walls of the villa were selling the same cloths and clay pots of olive oil as always. Everything looked just the same as it had been in the old days.

Don't look, said a voice in his mind. He knew that it was a mistake. But he pressed his hand against the cool outer wall of the main entrance. Lucius closed his eyes.

'One week, six days, three hours,' he said under his breath.

Ravilla, his uncle, had taken them away from the villa almost immediately. It had had to be sold, for all their father's money had disappeared with him. Their slaves and most of their possessions had been sold with it. Lucius's tutor Agathon, the cook Nicia, who had always made sure Lucius's dog had a good meal, the maids, the cleaners… they were all gone. Until now, Lucius had never known a day without them.

He had even lost his dog. Quin had been angry with him for being upset over a dog. But he couldn't forget Argos's faithful brown eyes. He had gone missing on the day the soldiers came – another victim of their family tragedy.

Lucius wondered if another family was living in the villa now. Who was looking at the murals on the walls? Who was sitting in his father's place? He hated every hour that passed. Every moment took him further from the last time he had seen his father. Visions of what had happened flashed before him. His mother, her eyes red-rimmed, leaving her home with a few treasured possessions. Her face when she saw their new home above the shops in the grotty Suburra district, which Ravilla had somehow found the money to buy for them. Quintus's blue eyes growing steadily colder as the days passed. 'Friends' avoiding them in the street. Everyone believing that his father was guilty.

Even more painful were the older memories. Studying with Agathon. Playing with the slaves' children in the free afternoons. His father stepping over the threshold at the end of the day. His smile when he saw Lucius waiting. His low, soft voice, reading aloud from his papyrus* scrolls. It gave Lucius an almost physical pain to remember his father's open, honest face. And yet, if the evidence was to be believed, he had been a merciless informer under the previous emperor, and had brought about the deaths of many honest people.

A sound came from inside the villa and Lucius's eyes flicked open. This wouldn't do. He had a message to deliver for Ravilla; his brother was still in the arena; and his father had gone. Those days were over now. He should be like Quin, and focus on the present instead of the past. He darted away, feeling as guilty as a slave caught dawdling.

---

* papyrus: paper made from Egyptian reed fibres.

As soon as Lucius had delivered the message, he slipped into a narrow passageway and leaned his head back against the wall. It was warm and rough, and somehow made him feel safe. He allowed his mind to drift back again.

Until Quin had made his terrible decision, Lucius had been sure that his father would return and clear up the whole mess. It didn't even occur to him that anyone might think differently. Not until the evening when his uncle had installed them in the cramped flat, and Quin had said, overly casually, 'You've invested money in a gladiator school, haven't you, uncle?'

'Yes,' Ravilla said, sounding surprised.

Lucius looked up at his brother, wondering where this was leading. Any conversation between his father and his uncle about the gladiator school had always ended in an argument. Aquila disapproved of Ravilla's gambling.

'Could you get me in?' asked Quin.

Everyone had laughed. It was a ridiculous question – of course Quin was joking. A free citizen of Rome – a lad who had barely taken the toga* – renouncing his citizenship and taking on the status of a slave? Only Quin's face remained serious.

* *toga: a long, loosely draped white garment, worn only by adult male Roman citizens. Quin, a teenager, is just old enough to wear one.*

'I mean it,' he said.

'Quin, don't mess around,' Lucius began.

'Shut up,' said Quin, and in that instant Lucius knew that he was deadly serious. His fun-loving boy-brother seemed to have completely disappeared.

'It's not an option, Quin,' their mother said.

But Quin didn't even reply to her. His eyes were fixed on Ravilla's face. Ravilla turned and stared out of the window at the dirty roofs of Suburra.

Lucius looked out too. He stared at the crumbling communal dwelling opposite them, with the large black letters painted on its walls, advertising living space. His thoughts were still swimming. He could not believe that in the space of a few days they had come from their beautiful villa, with its mosaics and slaves and portraits and library, to this cramped flat in Suburra.

They had been able to bring only a few personal belongings and a few pieces of furniture. The streets here were so narrow that his uncle's slaves had found it difficult to carry some of the furniture along them. The villa had contained more rooms than they had needed. Now they had just a couple of rooms above a stinking fast-food shop.

'This cannot be,' Ravilla said, his back still turned on his nephews.

'Yes it can,' Quin stated. 'Other citizens have done the same.'

'Men who have run into debt,' said Ravilla. 'Men with no other option.'

'*I* have no other option,' said Quin. 'You say I can't leave and join the army.'

'You can't,' said Ravilla for the umpteenth time. 'The stain of your father's actions – they would never accept you.'

'Very well, then,' said Quin. 'This family has to eat somehow. I can earn money, once I'm through the training.'

At last Ravilla turned to face Quin. The look on his face made shivers run up and down Lucius's back.

'I'll look into it,' he said quietly.

After Ravilla had gone, the arguments raged all night. First their mother and then Lucius tried to make him see reason.

'The minute you take that oath, you give up all rights,' Lucius said. 'You'll be treated as a slave.'

'There are advantages,' Quin said, not meeting Lucius's eyes.

'Oh yes, *fine* advantages,' said Lucius. 'The chance to die a gruesome death. The chance to suffer —'

'The chance to earn some money,' Quin snapped.

'You could become a teacher and earn money.'

'A pittance,' said Quin. 'In case you hadn't noticed, I have a family to support.'

'Not just you,' Lucius said. 'I'm the second eldest. I could do something – join the army…'

Quin wheeled around and gripped his brother's arm tightly. His blue eyes blazed. 'No, Lucius!'

'Why not? If you can be a gladiator—'

Quin shook him to shut him up. 'Weren't you listening? Thanks to Father, you'd never be accepted. Anyway, what's so bad about being part of a group? A group that stands for courage and loyalty and discipline? In the arena I could win honour and fame even greater than I could get in the army. I wouldn't have to fight more than two or three times a year. I'd learn military skills. I'd have fame, wealth—'

'*If* you won,' Lucius broke in, trying to stem the torrent of words. 'And if you didn't win? Oh, that's right – *death*.'

'I'm doing this for the family! I'm trying to save us from poverty and shame.' It was as if he had blocked up his ears to all sense or reason.

'You'll be their slave!' Lucius yelled. 'Do you realise that? They can keep you in chains if they want. You'll belong to them, and they'll never leave you alone for a second.'

'Only until I'm trained,' Quin went on, his voice softening. 'Once I've fought in the arena I'll have more privileges. And I'll eat better than most commoners. Why does this make you so angry? Get a hold of yourself.'

Lucius felt himself shaking, and tears pricked at his eyes. Quin was right – he had lost control. He blinked the tears back and mastered his voice.

'Father calls it "infamous",' he said. 'He'd never allow it.'

'Aquila's not *here*,' hissed Quin. 'And he stopped being my father the day he abandoned us.'

A shock passed through Lucius's body. He glanced at his mother, but she lowered her eyes.

And that's when Lucius knew that he was the only one who believed in his father's innocence.

CHAPTER II

'Hot sausages! Hot soup!'

The bellow of the street-stall vendor made Lucius open his eyes with a start. He had wasted time daydreaming. He pushed his memories to the back of his mind, storing them in the darkness. There was no time to look at them now. He hurried back in the direction of the school, feeling shaky and alone.

Quin was no longer in the training arena. Lucius looked around the side steps, expecting to see Quin's face among the others, intently watching the more advanced gladiators as they practised. His eyes scanned the faces, which were becoming as familiar to him as those of his own family. He saw the primus palus, Ruga, a Murmillo,* whose left eye and cheek were deeply scarred.

Lucius shook his head. A few weeks ago, he had no idea what any of these words meant. Now the language of the school was becoming as natural to him as breathing. Primus palus – 'first pole' – were the best gladiators in the school. And there were so many different types of gladiator – the Murmillones with their fish-shaped helmets, the Bestiarii animal fighters, the Thracians with their curved daggers... he was quickly learning to recognise them all.

Lupus and Bestia, the next in the palus hierarchy, were sitting together as usual, pointing at the gladiator that Crassus was training and no doubt discussing what he was doing wrong.

'He's not here,' said a voice behind him.

Lucius looked around and saw the slave girl again. Her voice was crisp and clear. He stared at her.

'Don't you speak to slaves?' she enquired.

'Of course I do. I...'

She waited, and he cleared his throat. He didn't have to explain anything to her, even if he knew how.

'Where is my brother?' he asked.

Her dark, straight eyebrows rose a little.

'The doctor is attending to him,' she said.

He took a step forward, but she didn't move.

'You're blocking my path,' Lucius said.

---

* *Murmillo, Bestiarius (plural: Murmillones, Bestiarii), etc.: some of these different kinds of fighters are described and illustrated on pages 206–207.*

28

'You've barely opened your mouth since you started working here.'

He took another step forward, but she didn't move a muscle. She was the same height as him, but he was small for his age. He was so close that he could smell her. She smelled of sawdust and sweat and blood.

'Excuse me,' he said in a low voice.

'I want to know what you are,' she said, just as if he hadn't spoken. 'They don't explain anything to us.'

'I am Lucius Valerius Aquila—'

'I know *who* you are,' she broke in. 'I was asking about your status. You come here every day. You're part of the familia.* You take orders from Crassus as well as your uncle. But you don't sleep here and they pay you money. So what are you?'

She had actually interrupted him! He was shocked into silence for a moment. The girl folded her arms and raised her eyebrows a little higher.

'It's a job,' said Lucius.

'What job?' she demanded. 'Sometimes you help us. Sometimes you run errands. Sometimes you assist the doctor.'

'It's just a job,' he snapped.

He was shaking. This girl was asking for answers that he didn't have. He had a job at the gladiatorial school, and that was all he knew. He did what he was told, and he received a small wage to add to the family's weekly income.

* *familia: a troupe of gladiators.*

29

'Let me past.' He shoved her aside and hurried towards the room where the doctor treated the wounded. He paused in the doorway. Quin was lying face down on the floor while the doctor bathed a map of cuts on his back. The doctor, Aelius Eumenes, looked up. Eumenes was Greek by birth, having grown up in the city of Pergamon. Lucius had heard that Eumenes had studied under the famous doctor and teacher, Aulus Cornelius Celsus, and that he'd learned his anatomy by studying the corpses of animals killed in the arena. He had the hard face of a man who had seen, perhaps, too much suffering in his life. He met Lucius's eyes, and for a moment Lucius thought he saw a flash of pity, but then it was gone.

'Ah, Lucius, just the person,' he said briskly. 'I could use your assistance here.'

'Lucius?' came Quin's muffled voice. 'Is that you? Did you see me fighting? How did I look?'

Lucius stepped forward and took the wet cloth that Eumenes held out to him. He dabbed gently at the dried blood around one of the gashes.

'Lucius?' asked Quin again.

'I saw some of it,' said Lucius. 'It looked… painful.'

'It was wonderful!' said Quin. 'I felt really alive, Lucius – I can't explain. Being in the arena… it's like having been asleep all my life, and then suddenly waking up.'

Lucius saw Eumenes' lips twitch, and Quin was silent for a moment. The atmosphere changed.

'I wouldn't expect you to understand,' said Quin, in a different voice.

Blood was trickling down Quin's sides in rivulets. It made Lucius feel sick. His body was covered with bruises of all colours from earlier training sessions. Lucius kept dabbing at the fresh cuts, pressing his lips together as hard as he could. What was the point of arguing? Quin had given his oath, and he belonged to the school now. Lucius had said everything he could to change his brother's mind, but it was useless. Quin didn't want to listen.

'They've assessed me and decided to train me as a Retiarius,' he said, unable to disguise the note of pride in his voice.

'Are those the ones with the big shields?' Lucius asked.

'No, that's the Secutores,' Quin said with deliberate patience. 'A Retiarius uses a net and a trident. I was hoping I'd get Retiarius. Crassus is the Doctor Retiariorum,* so he'll be training me, and he's the very best.'

'Right,' said Lucius, who in his mind's eye could still see Crassus punching Quin. 'Well, that's… good.'

'Would it hurt you that much to scund a bit pleased for me?' Quin demanded, half lifting himself from the ground.

Lucius sat back on his haunches.

---

* Doctor (plural: Doctores) Retiariorum: trainer of the net fighters.

'Stay still,' growled Eumenes.

Quin lowered his body again, grimacing as he did so.

'It's just that you make it sound like it's *all* fun, and it's not,' said Lucius, starting to bathe his brother's back again.

He was trying to make his voice sound reasonable and calm, but he had a feeling that it wasn't working. Quin let out a long sigh.

'Just have some faith in me, will you, brother?' he asked in a low voice. 'Just for once?'

Lucius felt his cheeks grow hot. He did have faith in Quin. He had always thought his older brother could do anything. But, this time, Quin was confronting mortal danger as if it were one of his games.

'You'll be all right,' said Eumenes, standing up. 'Another few weeks and injuries like that won't even draw blood. You'll have skin like leather.'

There's something to look forward to, thought Lucius. But he didn't dare to say it out loud. Quin stood up gingerly, and then grinned. Lucius grinned back at him. His brother hadn't looked this happy ever since their father had left. Even his startlingly blue eyes were sparkling like they used to when he had some new adventure planned out.

'Come on,' said Quin, putting one strong arm around Lucius's thin shoulders. 'Let's go home.'

'I can't just go, Quin,' said Lucius. 'I've got a job to do. And neither can you. Slave status, remember?'

Quin stared at him for a minute. Lucius wondered why he had never before noticed how cold his brother's blue eyes were.

'It's not my fault,' Lucius added.

'You didn't *need* to get a job here,' Quin said. 'I'll be earning money soon enough, and Uncle Ravilla takes care of us.'

'You're not earning money yet,' said Lucius. He didn't say anything about their uncle, but he remembered his father saying that Ravilla seemed to either have money to burn or be on the brink of poverty. It was strange that Quin hadn't picked up on that, when he was usually so clear-sighted.

'Lucius, step outside and get some air with your brother,' said Euemenes. 'I'll let Ravilla know you helped me treat him, and that I've suggested you both take a break.'

He left the room, and Quin glowered after him.

'He's just being kind,' said Lucius. 'Come on, let's go before Ravilla thinks of another errand for me.'

They made their way from the small room out to one of the narrow entrances used by the slaves. Lucius leaned back against the wall, but Quin seemed restless.

'Let's walk,' he said. 'We can take a few minutes.'

The streets were less busy than they had been earlier. Quin was walking carefully, as if each step hurt him. Lucius knew better by now than to offer sympathy. He wished that they were going home, and then winced at the thought. He had been thinking of the old villa, not the hovel where they were living now.

'I heard Mother calling out in her sleep last night,' he said. 'She was calling Father's name.'

'She should just forget him,' said Quin.

'I was starting to think she had,' Lucius went on. 'She never even mentions his name.'

'She's got more sense than you, then.'

Lucius was silent, but he felt as if his chest was burning with the effort of keeping his words locked inside. Quin gave him a sideways glance, and his eyes softened.

'I'm sorry,' he said. 'I know you're upset. But I'm just trying to be practical. Father's gone – and he's not coming back. He's crawled away somewhere like all the other traitors.'

'Aren't *you* upset, Quin?'

Their conversation was interrupted as they made way for two patricians* who were striding along together, their togas swirling, wafting scent towards the boys. Lucius recognised one of them; he had been to their father's villa many times in the past. Now his eyes passed over the two boys as if they had become invisible.

'There's no point in dwelling on the past,' Quin said as they continued walking.

Whether he was replying to the question or commenting on the patricians, Lucius wasn't sure. He

* *patrician: a member of an aristocratic Roman family.*

didn't know how to respond to a statement like that, anyway. Quin had always been the one with the quick reply or the witty retort.

'I don't want to dwell on the past,' Lucius said.

He paused, trying to think of the best words. Quin hadn't been so approachable since he'd started training at the school. He didn't want to break the spell.

'You've been different lately,' he said. 'More serious.'

'Finding out that my father's a filthy traitor has done that.'

'You really believe he's the Spectre?' Lucius asked.

Quin stopped and looked at him with a mixture of pity and irritation.

'Do you really believe he's not?' he said. 'Think about it, Lucius. The Spectre has been informing on people for years, and that means it has to be someone who has held an important position for a long time. It has to be a senator – how else would he have been able to report private conversations that happened inside the Senate to the emperor?'

'But Father *hated* the culture of informing on friends and neighbours,' Lucius said. Even as he spoke the words, he knew how weak they sounded.

'Yes, you're right,' said Quin sarcastically. 'The Spectre would be *so* likely to stand up for informers – as if that'd be the best way to protect his true identity. Grow up, Lucius.'

Lucius restrained the urge to give his brother a shove, and they started walking again. A darting shadow caught his eye. He turned to see a dog running by. It was large and heavy with brown fur – a Molossus, similar to his beloved Argos.

Everything was different now. Argos was gone, and Quin was different. He looked up at his brother and felt a wrenching sensation in his stomach. Before everything turned upside down, his brother had laughed easily and often. Now this grim expression was far more normal. Lucius couldn't understand it. Didn't Quin want to believe in their father?

'There's something I haven't told you,' he said. 'I haven't told anyone.'

'What?' Quin asked.

'That day – the day the soldiers came…'

'What about it?'

'I found a message in my room… from Father.'

'Oh, a letter telling his favourite son that he was innocent,' said Quin, his lips curling. 'How sweet.'

'Shut up and listen, will you?' Lucius said, wishing the wrenching feeling in his stomach would go away. 'It wasn't a letter – the soldiers would have found that when they searched. It was a secret message.'

'I don't understand.'

'I'd been reading something by Pliny, and the scroll was still lying on the table in my room. Father had underlined a phrase in it. I know that it was him. It wasn't underlined the last time I looked at it.'

'Typical,' said Quin. 'Always the same, you and him huddling together over a pile of dusty scrolls.'

'It said *Multi famam, conscientiam pauci verentur,*' Lucius went on.

Quin frowned. '"Many fear their reputation, few their conscience" – what's that supposed to mean?'

An image flashed into Lucius's mind: his father reading Pliny's work to him, explaining the things that he didn't understand. The man who had sat beside him, teaching him with such patience, could *not* have betrayed his friends and companions.

'It was Father's way of reminding me that he doesn't care about what other people do,' he said. 'He sticks to what he believes is right and wrong – he goes by his own conscience. He left it so that I would *know* he was innocent.'

'Lucius, that's an admission of guilt,' said Quin, sounding suddenly tired. 'He's just saying that he had his reasons, that's all.'

Lucius was speechless. For a moment he wondered if Quin had actually known their father at all.

'Our father believed in fairness and honesty and equality!' he said, his voice cracking. 'That message meant that he wouldn't have betrayed that, because he would have been betraying his own conscience.'

'Yes, and lots of people did, under the last emperor.'

'Not Father.'

Abruptly, Quin turned on his heel and started striding back towards the school. Lucius had to break into a half-run to keep up with him. It must have hurt Quin to walk that fast.

'Quin, why can't you just—'

'I've got to get back to the familia,' said Quin through tight lips.

'But—'

'I'll be in trouble.'

Lucius felt as if the weight of the world had dropped onto his shoulders. He watched his brother disappear back into the school, and then followed him inside.

Quin had already disappeared into the rooms the gladiators used for washing and sleeping. Lucius couldn't see him among the press of bodies and the clash of weapons and armour. He could hear the men making jokes and talking about their training session. Crassus spotted him and waved his arm.

'What are you standing about for?' he demanded. 'Think your uncle pays you to do nothing? Get outside and help clean up.'

The training arena would be spattered with blood and would need fresh sand. It would stink of sweat. Lucius started breathing through his mouth as he walked out between the columns. The slave girl who had spoken to him earlier was already there, scooping up the bloody sand and tipping it into a wooden bucket. She seemed to sense that he was there, and looked up, her eyes meeting his directly.

'Have you come to help or to watch me work?' she asked.

'To help.'

'Then take a bucket and a shovel.'

She jerked her head to one of the corner fountains, where another bucket was lying on its side. Lucius closed his eyes and pushed away his memories. *Our villa, our slaves, our life… it's all gone.*

He picked up the bucket and shovel, and set to work. Most of the blood, from earlier in the day, was brown and drying, but then he found some splashes that were still red and wet. Lucius paused and looked down at them. He felt sick. Then a hand touched his shoulder, and he flinched.

'It's not his,' she said.

He turned his head and met her steady gaze. For the first time, it looked friendly.

'How can you be sure?' he asked.

'I was watching. This patch belongs to Felix.'

Lucius must have looked blank, because she went on, 'He's the one who was laughing at you earlier.'

He bent down to scoop up the bloody sand, and when he turned again she was back at work. They made their way around the arena until it was clear. The girl put down her bucket, and Lucius walked over to her.

'What now?' he asked.

'Fresh sand.'

'You don't say much, do you?'

'I thought you didn't want to talk,' she replied.

There was a glint of humour in her eyes. Lucius had never shared a joke with a slave girl before.

'What's your name?' he asked, as they spread the fresh sand.

'I am Isidora,' she said, tilting her chin upwards a little as she spoke.

'Have you always worked here?'

'No, not always.'

Lucius waited. He had learned from his father that silence could sometimes be more useful than speech.

'I used to work in your uncle's household,' she said. 'I was glad when he sent me to work here instead. You're not like him.'

'What do you mean?' asked Lucius. 'What was he like to you?'

'What do you think?' she replied.

Lucius thought about his uncle's thin lips and sharp eyes.

'You didn't like belonging to him, then?' he asked.

'Do you?'

A jolt passed through Lucius's body. She was right. They all belonged to Ravilla now.

'But he's been kind,' he said. 'He's found us a place to live; he makes sure we have enough to eat. He —'

She stopped him abruptly by holding one slender, brown finger to his lips.

'You're a worker now,' she said. 'He owns you. And sooner or later, you'll see for yourself how he treats his possessions.'

They spread the rest of the sand in silence, and then picked up the buckets and headed towards the kitchen.

Lucius noticed that she lifted the buckets as if they contained nothing more than air. Her arms looked as powerful as those he had seen on a statue of the goddess Diana. His arms, by contrast, felt as if they were being dragged slowly out of their sockets.

'So it's better here, is it?' Lucius asked.

'If being a slave can ever be *better*.'

'My father was always – I mean – he taught us to be good to the slaves,' said Lucius, suddenly feeling awkward again. 'He said that it was one of the most important things you could ever do in your life – to be responsible for the life of another human being.'

'Then I wish I had belonged to him instead of his brother,' said Isidora.

Lucius was playing latrunculi* with his sister when Quin came home. Their mother jumped up and went to him.

'You're hurt again,' she exclaimed, seeing him wince as she touched him. 'I'm so glad you're allowed to sleep at home.'

'There are some benefits to being an auctoratus,' Quin said. He sounded tired, and he wouldn't meet Lucius's eye.

'A what?' asked Valeria.

'A volunteer gladiator,' said Lucius, standing up.

* *latrunculi: a popular Roman board game. Its name means 'highwaymen'.*

41

'Where are you going?' Valeria demanded. 'We haven't finished the game.'

'*I* have,' said Lucius. 'You won.'

He went into the room that he shared with Quin. He had only been allowed to bring what he could carry from the villa. He had the Pliny scroll with his father's message in it, a few other books, and a small box with things he had kept from his childhood. But Quin's side of the room was bare; he had brought nothing with him.

Lucius picked up the Pliny and sat on the end of his bed, but he didn't open it. He just stared at the label, remembering his father handing the scroll to him.

'Lucius?'

His brother came into the room and sat down on his bed opposite.

'We never used to argue, did we?' he said.

Lucius shook his head. He didn't trust himself to speak without his voice wobbling.

'I'm sorry,' Quin said. 'Things are bad enough without us arguing. I just don't want to think about... *him*...'

'Father?'

Quin clenched his fists and his whole body tensed. Then he relaxed.

'Even that word makes the anger come back,' he said. 'You know, Crassus told me to think about something that makes me angry when I fight. So...'

'You think about Father,' said Lucius.

CHAPTER III

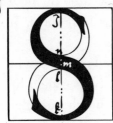o, what happened to your father?' Isidora asked, between spoonfuls of onion soup. 'He was a senator, wasn't he?'

They had been cleaning the barracks all morning. It was not a pleasant job. Lucius didn't know which he hated cleaning most – the filthy dormitories that the novicii gladiators shared or the stinking private rooms of the trained gladiators.

At last they had finished and had found something to eat from the kitchen. Lucius took a spoonful of his soup and grimaced. It wasn't the kind of onion soup that he was used to. This tasted like ditchwater.

'He was the best senator,' he said. 'A good man.'

'So why does everyone believe that he was some sort of traitor?'

Lucius would have minded most people asking, but somehow he understood Isidora. She was genuinely interested.

'What do you know about politics?'

'Not much,' said Isidora. 'What's the point of a slave knowing anything about anything? It's not as if we can vote.'

'But you know that the old emperor died?' Lucius asked.

'Yes, even slaves couldn't ignore that,' said Isidora with a grin. 'Vespasian died and Titus became the new emperor. The celebrations went on for four days. It was a lot of extra work.'

Lucius grinned too. At the time, he had only thought of it as a chance to have fun and relax. Now, when he looked back, he felt as if he had been much younger then – yet it was only a matter of weeks ago.

'Under Vespasian, our political system was full of informers,' he said. 'It was almost run by them.'

'Informers?' Isidora repeated. 'What did they give information about?'

'Anyone who was doing or saying anything against the law – or anything the emperor didn't like. It got so that people were scared all the time. My father said that there was a horrible atmosphere in the Senate. And there was one person they were all scared of – an informer they called the Spectre.'

Isidora frowned. 'Spectre? Like a ghost?'

'It was just a name,' said Lucius. 'It was because he seemed to be able to hear private conversations – it was as if he were invisible.'

'And now people think your father was this Spectre?'

'Yes, and it's ridiculous. Since Titus became emperor, he's been working hard to take apart all these networks of informers, and Father thought Titus was right – he hated the Law of Treason.'

'The what?'

'The Law of Treason,' Lucius repeated. 'It was a way of terrorising the political system. No one felt safe. If you said the wrong thing to the wrong person – that was it. And the Spectre was really good at it. He made people feel as if they could be caught out for even *thinking* the wrong thing. People were executed just on the strength of his word.'

'So Titus wants to get rid of the informers?'

Isidora was concentrating hard, following the explanation.

'Yes, and the one that they all wanted to find the most was the Spectre,' Lucius said. 'One day, soldiers turned up at the house. They said…'

His throat had suddenly dried up. The faces of the soldiers swam before his eyes. Isidora seemed to know that he needed a moment, and she looked away.

'They found things in his room that they said "proved" that he was the Spectre. He… he went missing. So everyone thought that meant he was guilty, and he was denounced in public as a traitor.'

'But you don't believe he did anything wrong?'

Her eyes were on him again.

'I *know* he didn't,' he said. 'I think that he heard about the soldiers coming and managed to escape in time. I don't... I don't know why he didn't stay and face them and say it was a lie. That wasn't like him. But he isn't a traitor.'

Isidora nodded slowly.

'You believe me?' he asked.

'You sound surprised,' she said. 'I trust you, that's all.'

Lucius *was* surprised. He had never thought of himself as being very good at inspiring confidence in other people. Quin had always been the one to do that. People seemed to trust him as soon as they laid eyes on him.

'Why?' he asked.

Isidora's cheeks went slightly pink, and then a little pale.

'Because you're my friend.' She spoke rapidly, as if afraid of what might happen to her. Lucius felt sure that she had never before called a citizen a friend. He felt pleased, and slightly embarrassed. He didn't know how to reply, but he wanted to show her that he felt the same. He decided to share something with her.

'When Quin took the blood oath,' he said, 'that was the moment when everything came crashing down.

Up until then, I told myself that Father would come back any day – that he'd explain everything and we'd go home and things would go back to normal.'

'But when Quin became a gladiator, you had to face the fact that everything had changed.'

'I think that the changes are only just beginning,' he replied.

They sat in friendly silence. Lucius thought about all the things that had already happened, and a shiver went down his back. What was lying around the corner?

'One day things will change for me too,' Isidora said.

Lucius heard a hard note in her voice, and when he looked at her he saw the determination in her eyes more clearly than ever.

'Isidora, is it…? I mean…'

She grinned at him. 'Stop stammering. Just say it.'

'Have you always been a slave?' he blurted out, before adding, 'Just say if you don't want to talk about it. Sorry. I shouldn't have asked.'

Isidora laughed.

'It's fine,' she said. 'Don't look so worried. I'm a slave; it's not exactly a secret.'

'So where are you from?'

'I was born here in Rome,' she said. 'But I am Egyptian. My parents were brought here from Egypt when they were young.'

Her brown eyes softened. Lucius thought of the stories he had heard about Egypt. The history lessons he had had from his father – how great Roman leaders of the past had fallen in love with Egypt. Even the famous Mark Antony had been bewitched by the place – and its queen.

'Egypt is a land of magic and mystery,' said Isidora, her voice slow and rich. 'Its people are fierce and proud and strong. My mother... she said I was Egyptian through and through.'

There was something in her voice that he hadn't heard before, but which he recognised immediately. It was like listening to the sound of something he had been feeling inside. He didn't have a name for it, but he knew that it made Isidora a closer friend than he had ever had; there was something they shared.

'Your parents aren't around any more, are they?' he asked.

She gave him a look that he couldn't fathom, and then shook her head. 'They're both dead.'

Lucius wanted to ask how they had died, but something about that look in her eyes stopped him.

'They told you about Egypt?' he asked instead.

'Yes,' said Isidora. 'Tales about home were bedtime stories for me.'

'You feel like you know it?' Lucius went on.

'Sometimes I dream about it,' she said. 'It's always the same. I dream that I'm walking through one of the markets. I can smell the spices from the stalls cooking food, and a heavy scent floating on the breeze. People are hurrying all around as I walk along – people who look like *me*, with dark skin and hair and eyes. And in the dream I'm free. No one can order me to clean up their vomit or wash their stinking clothes.'

The anger in her voice didn't scare him. It made him feel angry for her.

'You want to go to Egypt, don't you?'

He saw her jaw set into a hard line.

'I *will* go home,' she said. 'It's not just a dream; I think it's a premonition. I could buy a mule with the tips I'm saving – I'd only need 520 sesterces.'

'You believe that's possible?' he asked. 'To see the future in your dreams?'

Isidora laughed. 'I'm not as superstitious as your uncle,' she said. 'But however much I hate Rome, I grew up here, and I've learned that strange things can happen. Why are you frowning?'

Lucius hadn't realised that he was. He raised his eyebrows to clear his forehead.

'I didn't know my uncle was superstitious, that's all,' he said. 'I don't really know him very well. My father didn't… well… I don't think he liked him very much.'

'The more I hear about your father, the more I like him,' Isidora said.

'Was Ravilla that bad? As a master, I mean.'

'He's your uncle.'

Lucius almost choked on the last of his soup.

'I'm not going to run to him and tell him what you've said.'

Isidora shrugged. 'He was mostly just thoughtless,' she said. 'He could be cruel, but usually it was just that he didn't see us as real people. My father said that he was ignorant.'

'My father used to say that about him too,' said Lucius.

'I'm glad that he put me to work here, after my parents died,' she said. 'When I lived at his villa, I felt —'

She stopped abruptly.

'What?' asked Lucius. 'You felt what?'

'Scared,' she said.

CHAPTER IV

'He gets later every night,' said Lucius's mother.

Lucius glanced up from the game he was playing with his sister Valeria. The light was fading. His mother had been spinning, but now the spindle had slipped from her hands and she was staring into the middle distance. With a sudden jolt, Lucius realised that she did that a lot these days.

'He's working hard, Mother,' he said.

'Your turn,' muttered Valeria, jogging his arm to bring his attention back to the game. He looked at his mother's hands lying limply in her lap. He shivered.

'It's just at the beginning that he has to train like this,' he said, feeling as if he needed to bring her back from somewhere.

'It wasn't supposed to be like this,' she said in a faraway voice.

Lucius felt as if something was about to be said that he didn't want to hear. He stood up, ignoring Valeria's exasperated exclamation.

'I'll go back to the school – see what he's doing,' he said.

'Oh Lucius!' Valeria complained. 'It's supposed to be home time now. It's as if you and Quin don't even want to be here.'

'I'm going to fetch him,' said Lucius.

He pulled her hand off his arm and looked over at his mother. Her expression hadn't even changed.

Valeria folded her arms and threw herself down on the couch.

'Everything's horrible now,' she said.

Lucius slipped back into the school and made his way to the arena at the centre. It was strange being here in the evening. Slaves were hurrying past him, heading towards the gladiators' barracks with food and drink.

He glimpsed Isidora rushing along with a bowl and guessed that it was her job to bathe wounds tonight. They exchanged a quick smile, but there was no time to talk. He could already hear the yells and grunts of the gladiators who were still training, mixed with the voices of the trainers roaring their instructions. Crassus's voice rose more loudly than all the others.

'. . . and thrust . . . and cut . . . and slice – SLICE, YOU IDIOT! Quintus, come here and show him what I mean!'

As Lucius stepped out into the arena, he saw his brother wielding a large wooden sword and striking it against the tall wooden palus* that was sticking up out of the ground. Crassus was grimacing, which for him was almost a smile. Other novicii gladiators were watching, some of them panting heavily and sweating. Lucius had avoided watching his brother over the past few weeks, but now he couldn't take his eyes off him. The way Quin moved reminded Lucius of an animal. His muscles rippled under his skin, and his body had changed shape completely. His thighs, visible under the tunic he was wearing, looked as strong and thick as the pillars around the arena.

Ruga, the Murmillo with the scar that split his face in two, saw Lucius watching and lumbered towards him. He was a solid wall of a man, with a rank smell of blood, sweat and unwashed skin about him. Lucius took a step backwards as he drew closer.

'He's doing well, your brother,' said Ruga. 'Works hard. Gives as good as he gets.'

* *palus: a wooden post planted in the ground, used as a target for weapon practice.*

Lucius supposed that meant that Quin had been putting his quick wits to good use. He nodded, hoping that Ruga would leave him alone. But the huge gladiator clamped his hand on Lucius's shoulder, nearly making his legs buckle.

'He'll do well in the arena, when he's trained,' Ruga said. 'Good-looking. The girls will be writing his name on the city walls.' He gave a sudden grin that made his leathery face crinkle like burning papyrus. 'They used to write *my* name on the walls once. Can you believe that?'

Lucius nodded again, trying to stop his shoulders from hunching up around his ears. There was something about Ruga that made his skin prickle. *Why can't I be as relaxed as Quin when I'm talking to people?* he wondered for the hundredth time. *Why can't I be easy-going and think of the right thing to say?*

Quin was still practising on the palus, striking harder and faster, slashing at it with vicious strokes. Lucius wondered if he was thinking of their father. The clunk of wood hitting wood took on a sort of rhythm. Trying to forget the presence of Ruga beside him, Lucius gazed at his brother. He was incredibly light on his feet, considering his strength. Crassus was right – he would make a good Retiarius.

'It's like a dance,' he said to himself.

He was hardly aware that he had spoken aloud, but Ruga looked down at him.

'Retiarii are lightly armed,' he said. 'They have to

54

be fast on their feet. But it's more deadly than any dance *you've* ever done.'

Lucius noticed the mocking emphasis on 'you've' and looked away. He had lost his status when his father left the city, and it was only the fact that Ravilla had money in the school that made Ruga bite his tongue.

Quin's practice sword was a blur, and Crassus was urging him on. Lucius fixed his eyes on the palus. It was just a pole, but in his imagination the sword was a real one, and it was crashing down on his brother's body – smashing the life out of it. He turned to go and ran straight into a tall, toga-clad figure. Two strong hands clamped around his upper arms, and he found himself looking up into his uncle's piercing eyes.

'Hello, Lucius.'

'Hello, Uncle.'

'Watching Quin's training?' Ravilla asked. 'He's doing well. Every time I see him, he looks stronger. He'll have some great wins, when he comes to fight.'

Lucius kept gazing up at him, but he didn't reply immediately. What sort of a man was Ravilla really? The better Lucius got to know Isidora, the more he wondered. And yet Ravilla had always been accepted as part of the family.

'I don't care about Quin being good at fighting,' said Lucius. 'I care about him not dying.'

He noticed the way Ravilla's eyes never quite met his, and the way his thin lips curled when he smiled, like a sneer. Suddenly he seemed like a stranger.

'Bit of a mother's boy, aren't you?' Ravilla said. 'This was Quin's decision, Lucius.'

He strode into the arena before Lucius could reply. Crassus stopped Quin and walked over to greet Ravilla. Quin followed him, looking exhausted but happy. Lucius couldn't hear what they were saying, but all three of them glanced over at him and laughed. He pressed himself against one of the pillars and wished that he could melt into it.

Other novicii gladiators were walking towards him now, and some of them patted Quin on the back as they passed him. Lucius saw that some of the fully trained gladiators had been watching from the sides, and they were nodding to Quin as they walked back into the school.

Quin walked towards him, his body gleaming with sweat. He looked happy. Lucius felt as if he had to force his face into a smile.

'Have you been waiting for me all this time?' Quin asked. 'I thought you went home.'

'I came back,' said Lucius. 'Mother was worried.'

Quin's smile faded slightly. 'This is how it is now. She has to deal with it.'

They hadn't argued again. They hadn't spoken much either, but at least it had been peaceful. Lucius didn't feel like changing that just yet.

'It looks like you've made some friends,' he said, looking at the other gladiators who were still leaving the arena.

'I never thought I'd like them so much,' said Quin. 'But it makes you close to people – going through this together.'

'It's just that Mother—'

'Our uncle is going to come home with us tonight,' said Quin, talking over him. 'It's good you're here. We can all walk there together.'

Valeria was pleased to see her uncle, and her laughter and Quin's excitement made the little room more cheerful than it had been for some time. Valeria helped her mother to bring out some food and everyone ate. Quin and Ravilla talked about the school, and about the training, and gradually everyone else stopped talking.

'The training on the palus is really building up my upper body strength,' Quin said, flexing the muscles in his arm.

Valeria leaned over to feel his arm, and gave a little squeal of surprise. Quin laughed.

'It's like a rock!' she said.

Ravilla leaned back on the couch, took a sip of wine and looked around at the cramped little room. His eyes took in the cracked walls and the dark burn mark where a previous tenant's charcoal brazier had once stood. Then his gaze fell on his brother's wife.

'You're looking well, Caecilia,' he said.

There were dark smudges under her eyes, and little hollows in her cheeks. Lucius's uncle was either blind or lying.

'Thank you for the... snack,' said Ravilla, his eyes flickering over the meagre platters of cheap barley bread. 'It's lucky Quin's well fed at the school. He needs plenty of food to build up his strength.'

Lucius's mouth fell open, but Quin didn't even seem to have noticed that his uncle had insulted their mother. Ravilla, of course, was used to the best; his villa could easily be recognised by the clouds of greasy smoke billowing from the kitchens.

'I'm not used to living without slaves,' said Lucius's mother in a dull voice.

Lucius's eyes were fixed on Ravilla, willing him to apologise. His father would have asked him to leave. Even Quin would have said something – at one time.

Ravilla met his gaze and gave his sneering smile.

'Everything's different now, isn't it?' he said.

'It's horrible now,' said Valeria. 'I want to go home. How long do we have to stay here?'

She was looking at Quin, but he didn't seem to be listening.

'This is home now, Val,' said Lucius.

'What's happened to our villa?' she asked. 'I miss my room. I miss the gardens and the dining room and the marble pools and the —'

'Val, shut up,' said Lucius.

His mother's eyes were suddenly bright with tears.

'Valeria, your old home belongs to someone else now,' said Ravilla.

'But—'

'It was just a building,' said their mother in the same, dull tone. 'It isn't buildings that matter. It's people.'

'You see, Valeria?' said Ravilla. 'Be sensible like your mother.'

'But it's disgusting,' Valeria went on, her voice rising to a whine. 'People like us don't live in Suburra!'

'Julius Caesar grew up here,' said Quin.

'So what?'

'So stop being like this.'

'It's all right for you!' she said, turning on him with her hands on her hips. 'You're never even here. You don't know what it's like! Going to the public fountain to collect water like slaves, and then just sitting here smelling that disgusting food cooking below all day long, with no one to play with and nothing to do!'

Lucius was sitting on the edge of the couch, his elbows resting on his knees and his hands hanging down loosely. Valeria had always adored Quin – she had never spoken to him like this.

'Valeria, please,' said their mother.

'Well, you don't like it either,' Valeria muttered, pushing out her lower lip. She switched her gaze to Ravilla. 'Uncle, can you find me a job somewhere, like you did for Lucius? Please! I'd do anything – cooking, cleaning, working on a stall, as long as it gets me out of here!'

'Valeria, you mustn't ask such things of your uncle,' chided Caecilia. 'And you're far too young to work, anyway.'

'Maybe she is,' said Ravilla thoughtfully. 'But if you were to be there, too, Caecilia, working alongside her... Let me think about it.'

Caecilia looked down at her soft, pale hands. 'I've never worked a day in my life,' she murmured. 'I suppose times have changed, but I seem to find it harder than my children to accept it.' When she looked up again, her eyes were starred with tears. 'I can live with these changes,' she said. 'I can work, if I must. But Quin is risking more than any of us. I want you to keep my son safe, Ravilla. Can you do that?'

'Mother!' said Quin at once.

'He's strong and talented,' Ravilla said. 'He's going to be a great gladiator.'

'I just want him to live,' she replied, her voice suddenly hoarse.

Ravilla stood up. He walked slowly and heavily across the room until he was looking down at her. There was a long silence.

'I could speak to his trainer – the Doctor Retiariorum,' he said. 'He can... arrange it... for the training to progress slowly.'

Quin began to say something, but Ravilla flashed him a look that silenced him.

'Caecilia?' he said. 'Would you like me to do that?'

Lucius saw his mother nod, and Quin slumped

back into his seat, frowning.

'Consider it done,' said Ravilla. 'Now that my brother has gone, it is only right that I should take care of you all.'

'Are they still looking for my husband?' she asked in a low voice.

'He's left Rome; that's all they care about,' said Ravilla.

'You know that?' asked Lucius. 'Do you know where he is?'

'Trust me,' his uncle replied. 'We'll find him.'

'Why bother?' Quin spat out.

Lucius looked across at his brother and mother. Quin's arms were folded across his chest, and he seemed to be glowering at his own knees. Caecilia was staring into space, her face etched with lines of worry.

We're coming apart, he thought. *Father, where are you?*

CHAPTER V

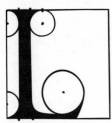ucius told Isidora about the argument at home, and the next afternoon she came searching for him with an expectant look on her face. Lucius was helping Eumenes by bathing some deep slashes on a gladiator's back. Eumenes noticed her first.

'Lucius, I think someone is trying to get your attention.'

Lucius looked up and saw Isidora standing in the doorway.

'Does Crassus want me?' he asked.

'Not exactly,' said Isidora.

'What is it, then?'

'Can you spare ten minutes?' she asked.

'Just tell me what—'

'Go, Lucius, for the goddess's sake,' said Eumenes. 'I can't concentrate while you're exchanging secret messages.'

Lucius put down the cloths he was using, wiping his hands on his tunic as he stood up. As soon as he reached the doorway, Isidora pulled his arm, and he saw that her eyes were sparkling.

'I've just seen your uncle,' she said.

'That's not something that usually makes you happy.'

'He's talking to Crassus,' Isidora went on. 'We should listen to what they're saying. They might be talking about your brother.'

'Look, I've got work to do here,' said Lucius, exasperated.

'Oh, stop arguing and just *come*!'

She grabbed his hand and dragged him down a corridor and out of the gladiator school.'

Lucius blinked in the dazzling sunlight. 'Where are we going?' he asked. 'We're not allowed to leave the building without permission.'

She rolled her eyes at him, and tugged him towards the public bath-house next door. Lucius was expecting them to be stopped by the porter, but he stood aside as they approached, and returned Isidora's smile. 'I sometimes work here as a cleaner during my time off from the school,' Isidora explained to Lucius as they entered the atrium of the baths.

Lucius had never been inside a public bath-house before. He gazed at the vast hall with its high, vaulted ceiling, mosaic floor and massive marble columns. On one side, a group of bare-chested young men were lifting lead weights and doing squats and press-ups. The atrium echoed with their shouts and grunts. On the other side was a row of small shops and salons. Traders were busy selling hot and cold snacks. Others were selling trinkets, including wooden models of gladiators. In one stall, a barber was trimming the beard of a rich-looking man in a toga. And in the small library and reading room next door, a scholarly-looking gentleman was peering at a scroll.

Isidora led Lucius towards another arched entrance, where a queue of visitors were waiting to hand their coins to the portly balneator, or keeper of the baths.

'Hello, Betto,' she called out to the balneator as she and Lucius bypassed the queue and slipped through the entrance.

'Mind how you go, Isi,' he smiled.

They walked down a crowded corridor that ended in a white-walled chamber – the apodyterium, or undressing room. The walls here were lined with low stone benches and pegs at head height, where bathers' clothes were hung. The room was spacious, yet full of clamour and loud talk, with people dressing or undressing, handing their clothes to attendants or demanding to know where their clothes had got to.

65

Isidora and Lucius fought their way through the throng of naked or semi-naked men and reached one of the four doorways leading off the apodyterium. This was the tepidarium, or warm room. It felt like a haven of tranquillity following the bustle of the apodyterium. Slender, graceful columns surrounded the rectangular pool like trees around a woodland pond. The walls were filled with frescoes of nymphs and pastoral scenes. The floor felt warm beneath Lucius's sandals, heated by the hypocaust system built underneath the bath complex. Through the steamy air, Lucius glimpsed a few men swimming lazily in the pool, while others lay on tables around its edge, receiving massages from slaves. The slap of hands on flesh, combined with the gentle splashing sounds from the pool, was very soothing to Lucius. He could smell the perfumed oil used by the masseurs; it reminded him of how his father used to smell after a trip to the baths, and for a few seconds he was transported back to happier times. Then Isidora broke into his daydream.

'They're not here,' she said.

'Who isn't here?' asked Lucius, forgetting why they had come.

'Crassus and Ravilla,' she replied, frowning at him. 'Who else? They were here not five minutes ago. They must have gone to the caldarium. Come on.' She led him down a short passage and into a smaller, plainer room, filled with clouds of steam. The caldarium was closer to the furnace that heated the hypocaust, and was much hotter. Lucius could feel his tunic becoming soaked with sweat. He could see several figures lying on tables. Slaves stood over them, rubbing oil into their backs, or scraping off the oil and sweat with a curved blade called a strigil. It was hard to identify anyone amid the gloom and the steam, but he thought he recognised his uncle and Crassus lying next to each other, speaking in a murmur.

Lucius and Isidora darted behind a fat pillar close to where the pair lay. They crouched in its shadow, listening as hard as they could to what the two men were saying.

'He's certainly the best we've had for a while,' Crassus was saying. 'Good stock, eh?'

Lucius heard his uncle's echoing chuckle.

'So you agree that he can take it?' Ravilla said.

'I never know what anyone can take until I try.'

'Don't be afraid to challenge him because he's my blood,' went on Lucius's uncle. 'That's all I'm saying – the boy could be a great gladiator, but I've seen you train lots of them, and I know you have to push them.'

'You've got a good eye for a fighter, Ravilla.'

They were interrupted by a sharp cry from another table, where a slave was using a pair of tweezers to pluck unwanted hair from a patron's back. 'Not so hard, you brute!' yelled the patron.

When Ravilla and Crassus resumed their conversation, it was to speak of other gladiators.

Lucius and Isidora slipped quietly out of the room. Back in the gladiator barracks, they walked slowly towards Eumenes's room.

'He meant Quin,' Lucius said. 'He told Crassus to push him harder.' He rubbed his forehead.

'I don't understand,' he said. 'Ravilla told my mother that he was going to ask Crassus to slow Quin's training down.'

'And he's said something different to Crassus.'

'Yes. Why would he do that?'

'Why do you think?'

Lucius recognised her tone. It was the same one his old tutor Agathon used to use, when he was encouraging his pupils towards the right answer. But in those days he had usually had a glimmer of what the answer might be. This time, he didn't have a clue.

Quin was practising at the far end of the arena. Lucius watched him working through his numbers – the classical series of moves that Crassus had taught him. He looked stronger than ever. Lucius could almost see the invisible enemy that he was battling.

Lucius didn't think that his brother had seen him, but Quin suddenly slammed the tip of his wooden sword into the ground and turned.

'See how I'm improving?' he said. 'Can you believe how much I've changed in just a few weeks?'

His blond hair looked almost dark, it was so unkempt and matted with sweat.

'My legs have actually changed shape,' he went on. 'Look.'

Lucius felt a sudden wave of irritation that took him by surprise. Could Quin think of nothing except his appearance?

'Never mind your legs,' he said. 'I've just heard something really strange. Our uncle's here, and I heard him telling Crassus to push you to your limits – to keep pushing you and challenging you.'

Quin picked up his sword again and made a few jabs at his imaginary opponent.

'So?'

Was he being difficult on purpose?

'*So* he told Mother that he'd do the opposite. He lied!'

'Just forget it, Lucius,' said Quin, tight-lipped.

'He's lying to us and I want to know why,' Lucius retorted. 'Don't you?'

Quin shoved him in the shoulder so hard that he staggered back and fell against the fountain.

'What's wrong with you?' Lucius yelled.

'*I* asked Ravilla not to tell Crassus to hold me back!' Quin shouted. 'Do you think I want to be known as the one who gets it easy? The one who doesn't get pushed because his uncle has money in the school? Do you know I'm the only auctoratus here? I'm the only one who volunteered to be a gladiator.

I'm the only one who doesn't sleep here like everyone else. But that wouldn't have occurred to you, would it? You're just a stupid little boy!'

'And you think *you're* a man?' Lucius shouted back. 'Did you ask him to tell Crassus to push you harder? Why would he do that?'

'Maybe because he thinks I can take it!' Quin bellowed, flinging the sword to the ground. 'Maybe because I'm *good*!'

'But did you know—?'

'Oh Lucius, shut up and stay out of my business! Ravilla understands – he knows this world. You don't.'

'But why would he—?'

'You've got a suspicious mind, just like Aquila!'

Quin was white to the lips, and their father's name seemed to echo around the arena and hang in the air between them.

'I'd rather be like Father than like Ravilla,' said Lucius at last.

Quin stepped up so close to him that their noses were almost touching. Lucius suddenly realised how much taller his brother had grown lately.

'And that's the difference between you and me,' he said, very quietly. 'What's the matter with you? What do you want? Do you *want* to believe our uncle's not trustworthy?'

'Of course not.'

'Do you trust me?'

'Yes, Quin, of course I do.'

'Then have some faith in my judgement, all right?' Quin said, relaxing his shoulders and stepping back. 'I've got to know him a lot better than you, and he just wants to take care of all of us. He doesn't have to do that.'

Lucius didn't reply, and Quin held his gaze.

'All right?'

'Yes,' said Lucius. 'All right.'

What else could he say? He wanted to shout in his face; he wanted to yell that this wasn't 'all right'. He wanted to shake Quin by the shoulders until he came back to his senses – until he turned back into the boy-brother Lucius recognised. He wanted to shake him until their life went back to normal – shake the last few weeks away – shake Ravilla away.

But he had spent all his life looking up to Quin, and now he couldn't find the words to explain what had changed. Quin was walking away from him, along a path that Lucius couldn't take, and every step seemed to be turning him into someone else.

That night, Lucius had a dream.

He was in the old villa, and everything was as it should be. The family gods were in their place, and sunlight filled every corner. He could hear birds singing, and his hands rested on Argos's soft brown head. Agathon was standing beside a fountain in the courtyard garden, planning his next lesson.

Lucius found himself walking towards his father's room, and he could see the familiar shape of Aquila's hunched, rounded shoulders as he pored over a scroll. Eagerly he hurried towards him, but somehow the way seemed to stretch further and further. He saw his mother reaching her hands out to him, but when he looked at her closely he saw that she was wearing a mask. Lucius tore at it and it came away in his hand, revealing Valeria's face, laughing hysterically.

He tried to run to his father, who had started to turn around, but suddenly Quin was in his way. Lucius tried to push him aside, but Quin's face seemed to melt like warmed wax, until it became Ravilla's face, laughing, with that strange way he had of curling his lips. Aquila started to walk away. Ravilla held Lucius's arms, stopping him from following. He tried to call his father's name, but he couldn't make a single sound. And now the walls of the villa were falling outwards, and someone was screaming.

CHAPTER VI

'K eep moving!' Crassus roared. 'A lash of the whip every time the sandbags hit you! Faster! Sharper!'

The novicii gladiators were dodging left and right, trying to avoid the rotating arms of the shield and dummy. Every time Crassus hit the shield, the dummy's arms swung around with sandbags attached to them. One wrong move and a single blow from a sandbag could bring a man down.

'Come on, you pack of fat, lazy dogs!' Crassus screamed at his trainees. 'Call this the peak of fitness? That slave girl could beat the lot of you! Duck, you idiot!'

A sandbag caught the side of Quin's head and sent him slamming into the floor of the arena. Lucius winced from his watching place. Isidora, who was behind him, gave a low laugh.

'Maybe I could,' she said. 'They have female gladiators too – some of the schools.'

'Not this one,' Lucius muttered.

He kept his eyes on Quin's face, trying to understand how he could have chosen this. He leapt up and dodged again, and was struck down again. There was blood trickling down his face, which was set hard with concentration.

'Why do you keep watching – if you hate it so much?' Isidora asked him.

She had moved around and was looking intently at his face. He flicked a glance at her and shrugged. He had stopped trying to understand how she could read his mind so easily.

'I just don't want to miss anything,' he said.

'You can't stop him from becoming… *that*.'

She waved her hand towards the older gladiators, who were watching the training from the side steps.

Lucius kicked the pillar beside him. 'It's like we're all turning into different people.'

'Your brother, you mean?'

'Not just him,' said Lucius. 'Mother hardly ever goes out, and Valeria's getting more and more…'

'More and more what?'

'I don't know the word for it,' said Lucius. '*Difficult*, I suppose.'

'What about you?' Isidora asked.

'What about me?'

'I suppose you think *you're* just the same as you always were?'

'Yes,' he said quickly. 'No. I don't know.'

'Oh, that's decisive,' she replied. 'Let me help you, aristo boy. You're nothing like the person you used to be. *He* lived in a fine villa and had slaves and a dad and status. *You* are little better than a slave yourself, your brother's a gladiator and you live in a slum. *And* your father's abandoned you.'

'Is this supposed to be making me feel better, Isidora?'

'All you do is think about how things *used* to be,' she said, suddenly looking angry. 'What good is that? Do you think my parents spent their lives crying and moping about the fact that they were once free Egyptians?'

'You talk about that all the time!' Lucius hurled back at her. '*You're* not happy being a slave!'

'Right, but I don't waste my time feeling sorry for myself,' she snapped. 'I know that one day I'll get the chance to go home – I'll see a way to go to Egypt. And I am not going to miss that chance because my eyes are too full of tears to see it!'

'So what am I supposed to do?' Lucius demanded. 'I can't make Quin stop training. I can't turn back time and stop him signing the blood oath.'

'Exactly!' she declared. 'So don't waste time feeling miserable about things you can't change. You think

Quin only ever thinks about himself – but you're just as bad!'

She turned on her heel and strode off before Lucius could think of a response. He realised that his mouth was hanging open and shut it with a snap. How dare she? She didn't know what she was talking about.

He turned back to watch Quin, but Isidora's words were echoing in his imagination. Was she right? Was he wallowing in the past when he should be… what?

With a shock of recognition, he saw Ravilla sitting on the steps opposite him. Lucius made himself start walking before he could think about what he was doing. The sounds of the practice arena faded away as he reached his uncle and stood beside him.

'Lucius,' said Ravilla, looking up and shading his eyes from the sun. 'Are you looking for an errand?'

'No, sir,' Lucius replied, feeling a little dizzy. 'I want to know what you are doing to find my father.'

Ravilla didn't reply for a moment. Then he stood up and looked down at him.

'You sound different, Lucius,' he said. 'Has something happened?'

'Like what?'

'That's what I'm asking you.'

'I just want to know where my father is,' said Lucius.

'We all want that,' Ravilla told him, placing a hand on his shoulder. 'We all want to understand why he did… what he did.'

'*If* he did it.'

A flash of annoyance showed in his uncle's face.

'Quin said that you are finding it hard to accept, but you have to remember that your father left. Why would an innocent man have run?'

Lucius didn't have an answer for that. He wondered if Quin had told him about his father's message.

'Will you tell me how you're looking for him?' he asked. 'Where you're looking?'

'I have friends in many places,' Ravilla said. 'I have sent messages – asked discreet questions.'

'But you're not telling me —'

'Lucius!' called Eumenes from the other side of the arena. 'I need you now!'

'You haven't been to see us since you told Mother that you'd make Crassus take Quin's training slowly,' said Lucius quickly.

Ravilla's expression didn't change.

'I know your brother has spoken to you about that,' he said. 'But your mother is not finding her situation easy. I only want to keep her from being upset.'

'Lucius!' called Eumenes again.

'I'm coming, Doctor!' Lucius called back. 'You think you can keep her from being upset by lying to her?'

'Things are not as black and white as you would like to think, Lucius. I'm trying to take some of the burdens from her shoulders.'

'What burdens?'

'The doctor is waiting for you.'

'*What burdens*?' Lucius said.

'Valeria is growing up,' Ravilla said shortly. 'Soon she will be ready for marriage. I can find a suitable match for her.'

Lucius started to say something, and then realised that he didn't have the right words. He turned and walked away, anger prickling under his skin like a rash. *He means us*, he thought. *We're the burdens*.

Lucius spent most of the afternoon running messages to the Forum for Crassus and his uncle, and, by the time he had sprinted through the narrow streets for the seventh time, he was too hungry and hot to care about anything except food. He bought something greasy and filling, smothered in fish sauce – which was all he could afford – and wolfed it down as he made his way back to the school.

He was about to go through the east side entrance, when he thought he heard a familiar bark. He spun around. 'Argos!' he cried. He scanned the street for his dog, but couldn't see him. His shoulders slumped. He must have imagined it.

He saw Isidora scrubbing the floor of the vestibule. She looked up at him and pushed some stray hair out of her face. She still looked annoyed with him.

'You've missed the excitement,' she said.

'What's happened?'

'A new novicius,' she said with a shrug. 'Looks more like a veteranus.* But what would I know?'

'Isidora…'

He wanted to say sorry. He wanted to explain that she had changed his thoughts somehow. But he didn't know how.

'I asked Ravilla what he's doing to find my father,' he said.

To his relief, she seemed to understand. The angry look left her eyes.

'That's good,' she said. 'Did you get an answer?'

'No.'

She raised her eyebrows. 'Are you going to keep trying?'

He smiled at her and walked through to the arena. She knew what he meant.

All the familia were in the arena, and Lucius had to climb higher in the stands to see what was happening. Crassus was in the centre, circling around with a gladiator Lucius didn't recognise, each of them with a rudis** and a shield. Lucius had seen this before. Crassus was testing him.

Their grunts echoed around the arena. Crassus lunged, slamming the wooden sword down, but each time it landed on the shield or was knocked aside. The

* veteranus: a trained fighter who has survived at least one combat.
** rudis: a wooden practice sword.

new novicius was pale and tall, with a broad chest and thick, muscle-bound arms. He looked as if he could have lifted Crassus with one hand. But there were other big, strong gladiators in the familia. The thing that made this man stand out was his hair. Lucius had never seen anything like it. It shone red and gold in the sun, like burnished metal.

It happened so quickly that Lucius couldn't have described it, even though he was watching. All he knew was that one moment Crassus was attacking the new novicius, and the next moment he was flat on his back in the middle of the arena. As soon as he caught his breath, he started to laugh. Lucius looked around and saw Quin leaning against one of the fountains with his arms folded. Lucius couldn't see him clearly, but he could tell that Quin was annoyed.

'So who *is* Rufus?' Isidora asked him the next day.

'I feel as if I've seen his face before,' Lucius said.

'Where?'

'I don't know,' said Lucius. 'But I... I don't know.'

They were standing at the end of the corridor they had just watched Rufus walk along.

'He barely talks,' said Isidora. 'He isn't like any slave I've ever known.'

'He isn't like any novicius I've ever known either,' said a voice behind them.

It was Quin. Isidora melted away to carry on her work; Lucius had never seen her speak to his brother.

'You don't like him?' Lucius asked.

Quin shrugged. 'I don't think he fits in. He's not part of the familia.'

'Do you recognise him, Quin?'

'Recognise him?' Quin looked puzzled. 'No – why? Should I?'

'No, probably not,' Lucius replied. 'I thought there was something familiar about him, that's all.'

They stared at each other in silence for a moment.

'You look taller,' said Lucius.

'You look thinner,' Quin replied, attempting a grin.

'So, what don't you like about Rufus?'

'He doesn't talk to us – the familia,' Quin said. 'He's from Britannia, but he won't even talk to his countrymen – you know we have a few Britanni in the familia.'

'You talk about the familia more than you talk about our family.'

'Maybe that's because being with them is a lot easier than being at home.'

Lucius was startled. 'What are you talking about?'

'It's not working,' said Quin, without meeting Lucius's eyes. 'Living at home, I mean. No one else does.'

'Yes, Quin, that's because they're *slaves*.'

'Don't get angry. Look, I've decided I'm going to sleep here from now on. It'll make me feel more a part of the familia.'

'And less a part of our family,' snapped Lucius. He didn't care about controlling his temper any more. How could Quin do this? 'Have you told Mother? Are you even going to bother?'

'You sound like a scolding woman, little brother.'

Lucius shoved him hard in the shoulder. 'Don't talk down to me, Quin.'

'It's hard not to when you say such stupid things.'

Lucius found himself shouting. 'You *have* to stay at home!'

'I don't have to do anything!' Quin yelled. 'It's all right for you! You do a few stupid errands here and you call it work! You have an easy life, and it doesn't make you part of the familia!'

'I don't care about being part of the familia,' Lucius replied, feeling sick. 'I care about *our* family.'

'I can't talk to you,' Quin growled. 'You don't understand anything.'

'No, you're right, I don't understand how you could decide to give up everything you had – I don't understand why you would choose this life! You're the one ripping our family apart, not Father! You hate him and now you've started hating us as well!'

'It's not like that!'

Quin grabbed his shoulders and shook him so hard that Lucius felt as if his brain was slamming against the inside of his skull. He couldn't get away – Quin was far stronger. He couldn't even shout. He felt as if he might pass out, and then Quin pushed him against the wall. Lucius's legs gave way and he slid downwards, sobbing with shock and pain. Quin staggered back against the opposite wall, panting, his eyes huge.

'I'm sorry—'

'Go – away,' Lucius stammered, trying to control the sobs. 'Don't – talk to me.'

'Lucius, I—'

'I don't want to hear it!' Lucius yelled.

Quin stood looking down at him for a moment longer, and then turned and walked away.

After the death of the hated Emperor Nero, the enormous palace he'd built in the heart of Rome, known as the Golden House, had been quickly torn down. Stripped of its marble, gold and ivory, it was filled with earth and built over. The Emperor Vespasian had decreed that a new amphitheatre should be built on the bed of the lake that had once lain in the middle of the palace grounds.

Lucius stared up at the near-completed Flavian Amphitheatre. He was awed by the towering, oval structure with is façade of brilliant white marble and its tiers of arches. Three storeys had been built so far, and the fourth was under construction. Enormous wooden cranes – remarkable constructions in their own right – had been erected to lift the heavy blocks of concrete into position on the topmost tier.

With an effort, he tore his eyes from the stunning sight, and continued along the Via Appia towards the much smaller timber amphitheatre, where games had been held ever since the Great Fire fifteen years ago had destroyed both of the city's amphitheatres. He passed through the shadow of the Colossus Solis, the only remaining relic of Nero's Golden House. And what a relic it was! The magnificent bronze statue soared over thirty metres into the sky. Nero had built it in honour of himself and placed it in the vestibule of his palace. Vespasian had added a sun-ray crown and renamed it after the sun god, Sol – turning Nero's vanity project into a gift to the city.

In a small wooden shack next door to the amphitheatre, Lucius found his mother and sister. After Valeria had begged him, Ravilla had found them some piecework, cleaning and repairing the costumes of gladiators and other performers in the arena. The interior of the shack smelled sharply of urine, the odour associated with all fulleries, where clothes were cleaned. It was a shock for Lucius, seeing his mother in these dingy, bad-smelling surroundings. A memory suddenly came to him of Caecilia reclining in her bedroom at their villa, while a slave applied powdered chalk to her face and another filed and painted her nails. Now her face, devoid of cosmetics, was set in a mask of grim concentration. Her delicate hands were red from toil as she stood bent over a tub, rinsing a grubby garment.

Valeria, by contrast, looked happy in her work. She was standing in a tub, stamping vigorously on a garment like a winemaker treading on grapes. Her tunic was tucked up, leaving her legs bare.

'Lucius!' she cried when she saw him. 'What are you doing here?'

'I came to see how you're getting on, Val,' he replied, trying to sound jollier than he felt.

He turned to his mother. 'Quin's not going to be sleeping at home any more,' he told her. 'He's going to stay at the school with the other gladiators.'

He had feared that his mother would be upset. But she merely carried on with her work.

'Mother?' said Lucius, after a long silence. 'Are you all right?'

'How can I blame him for not wanting to be there?' she murmured. 'I don't want to be there. Do you?'

'Is he going to be a famous gladiator?' Valeria asked.

'I don't know and I don't care,' Lucius retorted.

His sister looked startled – she wasn't used to Lucius being so blunt.

'You mustn't blame Quin, Lucius,' said Caecilia. 'He is a man now, and he has to find his own way to cope with what your father did. We all do.'

'*If* Father did anything wrong,' Lucius pointed out.

'Yes, Ravilla told me you said something similar to him,' his mother said, looking up into his eyes. 'Lucius, things are as they are. You will not be happy if you try to fight the truth.'

'But what *is* the truth?' he burst out. 'No one ever explains anything or tells us anything!'

Her stare became harder.

'The truth is obvious,' she said. 'Your father did something wrong, and when it was discovered he fled. We had to leave our villa and our life because our money and our status were gone. We are lucky that Ravilla is kind enough to look after us. This is how we live now, Lucius.' She raised the garment she was rinsing and showed it to him. 'This is the way things are. You are the only one still fighting to accept it. Why?'

He turned on his heel and stormed out of the shack. He didn't trust himself to continue the conversation and still be able to show her the respect he owed her. The anger inside him was building. Had no one *known* his father? The man he had known would never have stooped to spying and informing. How could his mother not realise that? Didn't she have eyes? Or had her marriage never been more than a convenient arrangement – had she never got to know the man her father had arranged for her to marry?

Lucius gritted his teeth. Ravilla had already started to think about finding a husband for Valeria – in two years she would be allowed to marry – and what sort of man would take on a wife with such a stain on the family name? Would his sister also marry a man whom she had never even got to know?

The following morning Lucius was out of bed before his mother and sister were awake. He dressed quietly, and tiptoed out of his bedroom carrying his calcei* in his hand. He found some bread and cheese for his breakfast and walked quietly out onto the street, where he put his feet into his calcei. One of the straps was getting thin – sooner or later it would snap.

He gobbled his food as he made his way along the dark, dirty street towards the Argiletum. He liked this road. It was lined with booksellers and cobblers, and he enjoyed peering through the bookshop doors at the walls lined with scrolls of papyrus. The smell of their workshops reminded him of studying with his father, and sometimes there would be loud discussions between the intellectuals who met there, which he would long to stay and hear.

As he passed a cobbler's shop, he glanced down at his calcei again. They were looking old and worn already – unused to the wear and tear of his work at the school. How long would it be before he couldn't wear them any more? The red, fine leather calcei would be replaced with a coarse brown pair that would fit badly and hurt his feet. He didn't care about that – most of his body ached all the time now

---

* *calcei (singular: calceus): outdoor shoes made of leather.*

anyway, and he was getting used to it. But it would be one more thing to separate him from his old life.

He emerged from the Argiletum into the Forum as dawn broke and made his way towards the school. Even though it was so early, the sun was already beating down on his head. The gladiators were awake and training – he could hear their grunts and shouts as he walked into the school.

Crassus was standing just inside the arena, but Lucius didn't report to him immediately. He saw Quin practice-battling with Ruga, and then he noticed the new novicius, Rufus, standing by one of the fountains. For some reason he wasn't taking part in the practice. Instead, he was gazing intently at Quin.

Lucius looked at his brother and then back at Rufus. The tall, angular gladiator looked as motionless as a statue. Why was he staring at Quin like that? A sudden yell made Lucius jump.

'Lucius, are you paid to watch the training?' Crassus had turned and seen him. 'Go to the kitchen and ask if they have any jobs for you. I'll have some messages to send later.'

Lucius slipped down the side of the arena and into the kitchen, where the gladiators' food was prepared. Isidora was there, stirring a large pan. She saw him and wrinkled up her nose.

'The doctor's brew,' she said. 'It stinks.'

'You mean that dark drink they all take?' Lucius asked. 'What is it?'

'Bone ash,' said Isidora, ladling up a spoonful and holding it out to him. 'Want to try?'

'Ugh, no thanks,' he said, backing away as a foul stench hit his nostrils. 'Crassus told me to come and find something to do.'

'Make some more of the barley broth, if you're looking for a job,' said Isidora. 'We have to feed the brutes soon. First meal of the day. Make them big and strong.' She held out an arm and flexed her muscles. 'And fat!'

Lucius had made the broth before. It smelled bad, but not as bad as the potion Isidora was cooking up. Other slaves dashed in and out of the kitchen as he poured barley into a pan and added water.

'Quin's not going to be sleeping at home any more,' he said.

'I know,' said Isidora irritatingly. 'Posca heard you fighting.'

Lucius felt his cheeks growing hot. 'So we're being gossiped about now?'

Isidora gave him a friendly nudge. 'As you always were, aristo boy. Except that now you get to hear about it. Forget it. Don't you have bigger things to think about than what Posca whispered to me while we were feeding the gladiators last night?'

As usual, she had the knack of popping the bubble of anger in him.

'Everyone seems to think we should just get on with life the way it is now – not question it,' he said.

'Even my mother would rather fold her hands in her lap and accept it.'

He glanced at Isidora, who leaned over the pan, sniffed the mixture and pulled a face.

'If they want to think like that, you won't change their minds,' she said. 'But if I thought that I would be living like this all my life, I think I would steal one of the gladiators' swords and fall on it.'

Lucius smiled and hoped that she was joking. She walked over to the archway that led out to the arena.

'Is Rufus still watching?' he asked.

'No, he's fighting Lupus now,' she replied. 'He's good.' Something in her posture changed – her whole back seemed to stiffen.

'What is it?' Lucius asked.

'Girl, get back to work!' bawled Secundus from the other side of the kitchen.

Isidora darted back to the steaming pan and continued to stir. Secundus was a fair man, but no one wanted to be on the wrong side of him.

By the time the food was ready to be served, the gladiators were already in the mess hall, waiting impatiently. Isidora and Lucius handed the food around and then gave each gladiator a small cup of the doctor's brew. When he handed it to Rufus, the pale newcomer stared at it in silence.

'Drink,' grunted Ruga beside him.

'What is it?'

Ruga turned to look at him – very slowly. The scar on his face seemed to twist into his scowl, so that his face was one cruel gash. Lucius shuddered, but Rufus seemed unaffected.

'Drink,' Ruga growled again. 'Makes you big and strong.' He made a strange choking noise, and after a moment Lucius realised he was chuckling. Somehow it was even scarier than his scowl. Rufus swigged the drink in one gulp and handed the cup back to Lucius. His eyes slid across the room and fell on Quin.

'Why was he staring at your brother like that?' whispered Isidora as they left the mess hall.

'We should ask him,' said Lucius.

'Great idea,' said Isidora with a laugh. 'I volunteer *you* to question the strange, enormously strong, new gladiator.'

Lucius tensed up for a moment and then relaxed. He was starting to understand her humour.

'Isidora, what did you see earlier on – when you were looking out into the arena?'

'Oh…' she shrugged. 'It was your uncle – I just wasn't expecting to see him, that's all.'

They took the dirty cups back to the kitchen.

'I'm starting to hate seeing him here,' said Lucius. 'The other day he was walking along with Quin, and they were so close that their heads were almost touching. It was… I don't know…'

'Scary?' Isidora suggested, starting to wash the cups and flinging a drying cloth at him.

'I suppose.'

Isidora looked around and then lowered her voice. 'Ravilla's a bad man,' she said. 'You know that, so everything he does seems suspicious. I understand, believe me. But what harm can come of him talking to his nephew? I think you're worrying too much. Quin explained to you why he lied to your mother.'

'It's this whole familia thing,' said Lucius, drying a cup rather too vigorously. 'It's as if the more time Quin spends here, the more angry he seems to be with us – our family, I mean.'

'It sounds as if it's Quin you're worried about, not your uncle.'

'I suppose,' he said again. 'And Ravilla's been very kind to us, really. He's letting us stay in one of his houses free of charge, and he found me this job.'

Before Isidora could reply, Crassus put his head around the doorway and beckoned Lucius to follow him.

Crassus had a list of messages he wanted Lucius to deliver. He was in a good mood, so Lucius knew what to expect. The trainer enjoyed finding out what hurt people. He would seek out a weak point and then jab at it until he got a reaction. It was one of the ways he controlled the gladiators, and he began on Lucius as they crossed the arena.

'You're an excellent delivery boy,' he said.

'Amazing the new *talents** that have been discovered in your family lately, isn't it?'

Lucius felt his hackles rising. *How does he do it?* He longed for the words – and the status – to silence the man.

'No need to look so peevish, boy,' Crassus laughed. 'Your brother's very talented. Wonderful what an aristo can do if he puts his mind to it.'

He was talking about Aquila. Lucius knew it, and Crassus knew he knew it. But he would never admit it. Lucius drew in a long, slow breath.

'I should go, if you want these delivered quickly,' he said.

The tiny, mocking light that had been in Crassus's eyes melted away. *No luck*, thought Lucius with venom. *This fish is not biting*.

'It won't be long before your brother completes his training,' said Crassus. 'He'll soon be a tiro** – ready for his first fight.'

Lucius turned and walked away. He didn't care if he was being rude. He didn't care if he lost his job. Watching the training sessions was bad enough – how could he watch while his brother walked into an arena and put his life in the hands of a baying mob? It was all very well for Quin to say that gladiators were rarely killed – *some* of them died, and that was too many.

* talents: this is a joke – a talent was a large sum of money.
** tiro: a beginner.

PART TWO

TIRO

CHAPTER VII

ucius, someone's coming!'

Isidora's urgent hiss brought Lucius shooting out of the barracks. There were footsteps approaching along the corridor. They darted out into the arena, Lucius's heart battering inside his chest.

'Did you find anything?' asked Isidora.

'I didn't have the chance!' Lucius exclaimed. 'What would they do if they found us in there looking through Rufus's possessions?'

'They'd beat *me*,' said Isidora. 'I don't know about you. They'd probably just send you to your uncle. *He* might beat you.'

'I'd like to see him try,' said Lucius, though he privately wondered how he could stop him. 'Anyway, can you please not sound so relaxed about beatings?'

'Sorry,' said Isidora with a grin. 'Am I offending your patrician feelings? Didn't your father ever beat you?'

'Of course not,' said Lucius. 'He… he didn't believe in pain as a way of controlling people.'

'Sometimes it's the only way.'

'Who told you that?'

'No one *told* me,' said Isidora. 'I learnt that particular lesson for myself.'

Her face had taken on the closed expression that Lucius had come to recognise. It meant that she wouldn't answer any more questions. It was the kind of expression that Crassus would have pounced on, but Lucius didn't want to jab at her raw feelings. He wasn't sure that he wanted to know about them.

Rufus had only been there for a short time, but he had already become one of the best novicii in the school's history. Before his arrival everyone had been calling Quin the rising star of the school, but now it was Rufus they were talking about. Lucius rarely spoke to his brother, but he could tell that Quin was angry to have lost the little bit of status he had gained. Rufus said little and watched Quin like a hunter.

That morning, Isidora had gone to clean the barracks and found Rufus looking through Quin's meagre possessions. When she told Lucius, he had decided to search Rufus's quarters… but he had been interrupted.

'What were you hoping to find, anyway?' she asked.

'I don't know – something to tell me who he is.'

'It *is* strange how interested he is in Quin,' Isidora went on. 'What do you think he wants?'

'That's what I have to find out,' said Lucius. 'Our family was powerful and important, and we had enemies just like anyone else. What if someone wants revenge on Father by hurting Quin?'

'It'd make more sense to hurt *you*,' said Isidora, looking thoughtful. 'Sorry, but it's true. Quin's watched all the time – he's a lot harder to get to than you are. Why would someone bother sending Rufus into the school when they could just grab you any time you were running an errand in the city?'

'You're right,' said Lucius, trying to clear his thoughts. 'But I can't shake off this feeling that I've seen Rufus before. I have to know what he wants.'

Saying it out loud made him feel more determined. Most of the gladiators were practising their individual numbers, but a few were watching from the steps, and Rufus was one of them. Lucius made up his mind to ask him straight out what he was doing at the school.

'Lucius, what are you doing?' exclaimed Isidora as he turned and headed towards the steps. 'Lucius!

You're not seriously going to question him?'

She had to run to stay alongside him. He didn't take his eyes off Rufus. 'I want to know how he'll explain himself.'

She tried to grab his arm to stop him, but he shook her off and only stopped when he was standing in front of the red-headed gladiator.

'Rufus, I need to ask you something.'

The redhead's pale blue eyes rolled slowly upwards to look at Lucius, then dropped to the arena again.

'I want to know what's so interesting about my brother,' Lucius went on. 'Why were you searching through his things this morning?'

'I was not.'

'I saw you,' said Isidora at once.

Lucius hadn't realised that she had followed him and her voice made him jump. Rufus didn't even look at her.

'I was not,' he said again.

'But I saw you – I know what you were doing!' Isidora was too indignant to be scared.

'What's your interest in Quin?' Lucius asked, when it became clear that Rufus was not going to reply.

There was another long silence, except for the roars and grunts from the arena.

'Where have I seen you before?' Lucius tried. 'I know your face.'

'Come on, Lucius, he's not going to answer us and we can't make him,' said Isidora, tugging at his elbow.

'But—'

'All of you get down into the arena now!' bellowed Crassus, drowning out Lucius's words. 'Halt all training!' The other trainers came to join him at the centre of the arena, and the novicii and veterani gathered around them. Rufus stood up and walked past Lucius without a word.

'That went well,' said Isidora. 'Come on, Secundus will be wondering where we've got to.'

'Wait,' said Lucius. 'I think something's going on.'

'I've always told you that if you work hard for me, I'll reward you,' Crassus was saying. 'Most of you don't listen to me—' this drew a ripple of laughter '— but sometimes a novicius comes along who shows the kind of dedication and talent that trainers like us dream about.'

Lucius felt as if his heart had suddenly leapfrogged into his throat. He knew what was coming.

'What's going on?' Isidora whispered.

'I think he's going to make Quin a tiro.' Lucius's lips felt numb as he spoke, and Isidora looked shocked.

'He wouldn't – it's too soon!' she said. 'If he's made a tiro then he'll have to fight in the next spectacle, and that's next week!'

Lucius sought out Quin in the little crowd around the trainers. His brother was flushed with pride and excitement – Lucius knew that look of old.

'We have a novicius here who has more skill in his little finger than many experienced gladiators I've seen,' Crassus went on. 'So this is a warning to all of you. From now on I expect every novicius here to aim for the standards Rufus achieves. I want every veteranus to know that there's a new talent in the school. There's always someone bigger and better than you, lads, remember it. I don't care how popular you are with the ladies!'

Quin's face had fallen at the mention of Rufus, and his whole body had stiffened. He looked somehow smaller. Several of the other gladiators had gathered around Rufus and were slapping his back and joking with him. Others, like Quin, looked bad-tempered and resentful.

'Much to my disappointment,' Crassus went on, 'Rufus will be fighting as a Thraex,* so Doctor Maximus will have the pleasure of training him. But I will be keeping a close eye on his progress.'

'Why would he do that?' Lucius asked. 'Won't it make enemies for Rufus?'

'Some,' Isidora agreed. 'But it will make the others work harder, and some of them will be pleased for Rufus. See Aprilis there, patting him on the back? He is one of the decent ones. He never gets noticed, but he's good and reliable.'

'He looks young,' said Lucius, staring at the dark-haired Aprilis, who was in his full Retiarius outfit.

'He's seventeen,' said Isidora. 'He's Egyptian, like

---

* *Thraex: a gladiator armed like a Thracian. The Thracians were a warlike people from Central Europe.*

me.' Lucius glanced quickly at her, but she was looking away.

'You're probably right about it making them work harder,' Lucius went on, uninterested in the young Egyptian man. 'Quin looks ready to start fighting now.'

Crassus set the trainers to work again, and then said something to Quin, who instantly unclenched his fists and looked pleased. Crassus glanced around and saw Lucius and Isidora watching.

'What are you two standing about for?' he roared. 'Girl, fetch me a net and a trident. It's time for Quintus here to find out what fighting as a Retiarius is really like. Aprilis, he'll be training with you. Lucius, do we pay you to spectate? Get to work!'

Isidora darted away to obey, and Lucius followed her swiftly, conscious that his brother's eyes were on him. He decided to speak to Quin abut Rufus as soon as he could. If the new gladiator was planning something, Quin ought to be ready for him.

However, the gods were not on Lucius's side. It proved impossible to speak to Quin that day. He barely left the arena, and when he did Ravilla appeared, seemingly out of nowhere, and sent Lucius on an errand that took him to the other side of the city.

Lucius spent the day running to and from the Forum, the messenger bag around his waist heavy with scrolls and wax tablets. The streets were crowded. A funeral was picking its way through the throng of carts and chariots. Hawkers were selling or bartering goods from every corner of the empire. Sulphur matches were swapped for bits of broken glass. Lucius spotted a man who was allowing vipers to bite him, just to demonstrate the antidote that he was selling to the crowd.

Turning to cross the road, Lucius's path was blocked by a team of sweating slaves moving blocks of marble for the new amphitheatre.* It had been under construction for seven years – Emperor Vespasian hadn't lived to see it, and Lucius wondered if it would ever be finished.

By the time the gladiators were beginning their evening practice, the bones in Lucius's feet felt like knives cutting into him. He limped back into the school, checked that he had delivered all his messages and then leaned against one of the arena pillars. He lifted first one foot and then the other to give each a rest, and wished that he hadn't bothered – it made them feel worse.

People were dashing back and forth behind him – gladiators returning to the arena, slaves going about their duties. Quin was still in the arena, carrying the trident, net and short sword of the Retiarii. Lucius thought that he looked awkward compared to Aprilis – it was obvious that he wasn't used to them. The galerus, the metal guard which was tied to his left

---

* *new amphitheatre: the Amphitheatrum Flavium, begun in AD 72 and finished in AD 80. It later became known as the Colosseum, after a colossal statue of the emperor Nero which stood nearby.*

shoulder to protect his head, made him look off balance and ungainly. He was standing behind Aprilis, copying his moves with his back to Lucius. It looked as if he would be there for a while.

I'll talk to him tomorrow, Lucius decided, refusing to admit that he was glad of a reason to put off talking to his brother. Crassus saw him and waved to say that he could leave. Lucius looked across at the kitchen entrance but couldn't see Isidora, so he turned around and headed home.

It seemed a longer walk than usual. Every step sent stabs of pain shooting up through his feet. He kept his head down, focusing on putting one foot in front of the other. The voices around him, rising and falling like waves, seemed to merge into a buzz that filled his head. He registered the greasy smell of street food, but he was too tired to feel hungry. All he wanted to do was to lie down.

By the time he reached the flat, he felt as if his feet were stuck to the ground, and it took all his strength to lift them. He dragged himself up the stairs and stumbled towards his room. The stale smell of fried beans and raw cabbage in vinegar still hung in the air.

'Lucius—' began his mother, half rising from the couch where she was working with her spindle.

'Tired... bed...' he mumbled. Five steps more – four – three – and then a rapturous feeling of relief as he collapsed onto his bed. Groaning, he unstrapped his calcei and dropped them onto the floor. His feet throbbed. As he took off his messenger bag, the flap fell open and he glimpsed a brown wooden frame – the edge of a wax tablet.

Lucius's stomach gave a horrible lurch. He had forgotten to deliver one of the messages.

He forgot about the pain in his feet – he just felt sick and hot. But when he pulled the wax tablet out of the bag he stared at it in astonishment. His name was written at the top. Lucius would have recognised the writing anywhere. He had watched his father writing for as long as he could remember.

His breathing seemed very loud in the still room as he looked at the message carved into the wax. There were just two words, written by the same hand.

'*Carpe ðiem,*' Lucius read aloud.

He stared at the words. 'Seize the day'? Why would his father be writing to him to tell him that? How had the message got into his bag? Had his father been into the school? It seemed almost impossible – every visitor was seen. Was he imagining his father's handwriting? Was he seeing things?

He wished he still had Argos by his side. His dog had always listened when he needed to talk. The letters swam around and blurred, and Lucius realised that his eyes were closing despite himself. He tried to force them to stay open, but sleep was overpowering him. Just before he fell back onto his bed, he tucked the wax tablet under his body. Until he understood what it meant, he didn't want anyone to know about it.

CHAPTER VIII

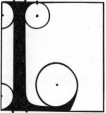ucius woke up with a start, his mind already racing. The words *'Carpe diem'* were drumming through his thoughts.

Who could he talk to about this? His mother? Impossible – she didn't want to think about anything. She would refuse to listen, or simply not hear him. Valeria was too young and talkative. She would be sure to tell the first stranger she saw that they had heard from Aquila – too dangerous. Besides, what useful advice would he get from a ten-year-old who still played with a hoop?

Quin was the obvious choice, but Lucius had barely exchanged two words with him since their argument. Also, Quin was liable to fly into a rage at the mere mention of Aquila's name.

He could talk to his uncle, but would Ravilla be obliged to report any contact to the Senate? Lucius had seen for himself how good a liar he was. What if he promised to keep quiet and then told someone?

No, there was only one person he wanted to confide in. He swung his legs over the side of the bed and winced as his feet touched the floor. Even after a night's sleep they were still sore. Standing up, he felt his way over to the window and threw open the shutters. It was still dark, although the sky was lightening by the minute and dawn would soon break.

There was no sound from within the flat. In the villa, slaves would have been hard at work by this time, and his mother would have been walking among them, making sure that they were following all her orders. Lucius could almost hear their cries of 'Yes, domina'* as she briskly checked their work. Now she hardly seemed like the same woman.

Sure enough, no one was up when he left. However, the school slaves were all hard at work when Lucius arrived. The clatter of buckets, brooms and ladders filled the air and Secundus was scurrying from room to room, calling out instructions. The gladiators were in the arena, stretching and preparing to train. For the first time, Lucius thought he

* *domina: mistress.*

understood how Quin could feel more at home here than with his family.

He hurried along the edge of the arena, peering into the rooms. Slaves were hard at work in each one, scrubbing, dusting and sweeping. He found Isidora in the latrine with a mop, cleaning the floor. A bench ran along each wall. The benches contained a row of round openings. On the floor between the benches ran a narrow channel along which water flowed, fed from a pipe in the far wall. A couple of bowls sat next to the channel. One of these contained fresh water so that patrons of the latrine could wash their hands. In the other bowl stood a set of spongiae – sponges stuck on the end of long sticks, for latrine users to clean themselves with. They were supposed to clean the spongia in the channel of running water after use, but some didn't do this – or do it very well – and it was often the unfortunate task of a slave to do it for them.

'Morning,' Lucius said to Isidora. 'I need to talk to you.'

'Can you help me clean at the same time?' she asked, nodding towards a mop leaning against the wall. 'Secundus woke up in a bad mood and decided the whole school needs a thorough clean.'

Lucius picked up the mop, dunked it in the channel and began to clean one of the corners of the room.

'When I got home last night, I found a message in my bag,' he began.

Isidora gave an explosive little laugh. 'You forgot

to deliver something for Crassus? I wouldn't want to be you.'

'That's what I thought at first,' said Lucius, 'but I was wrong. It was a message for me.'

'I don't understand – someone put a message in your bag? Why didn't they just speak to you? That's strange.'

'Isidora, it's more than strange,' he replied. 'It's in my father's handwriting.'

She stopped mopping and stared at him with her mouth open.

'What does it say?'

Before Lucius could tell her, a couple of gladiators came in, hoisted up their tunics, sat down on one of the benches and did their business, while continuing with their conversation.

Lucius and Isidora carried on cleaning the floor. He sensed her glancing at him every few seconds, desperate to know about the message from his father.

When the gladiators had finally gone, Lucius reached into his bag for the message and handed it to her.

'*Carpe diem*?' She looked disappointed.

'It means "Seize the day",' Lucius explained. 'It means that he wants me to do something. But what?'

'I don't understand,' murmured Isidora, still staring at the wax tablet. 'How could your father have been close enough to have put something in your bag without you noticing him?'

'I don't know. It's a crush in the city, though, and I was in the Forum a lot yesterday. Someone could have slipped it in as I passed them.'

'Did you take your bag off yesterday?'

'No,' said Lucius, shrugging. 'I was running messages all day – and I hardly ever take it off anyway.'

She handed the wax tablet back to him.

'Why would your father have made contact with you like this?' she asked. 'Why wouldn't he write a clear message – why these two words?'

'Do you remember what I told you about the message he left me in the scroll?' Lucius said. 'He did that because he didn't want anyone but me to find it. Maybe this is the same – maybe he's trying to tell me something but, in case anyone else found it, he had to write in a sort of code.'

'Yes, but it's no good if you don't understand the message,' said Isidora. 'Could it be a trick? What if someone is trying to see if you know where he is?'

'They'll be disappointed,' Lucius said with a sigh.

They stared at each other. Lucius guessed that she was running everything over in her mind, just as he was.

'Why haven't you finished in here?' Secundus roared from the doorway. 'Get to work or Crassus will sell the pair of you! I don't care who your uncle is!'

He disappeared again and Lucius heard him bellowing at Posca. He grinned and they finished mopping up the rest of the floor.

'Did your father ever use that phrase to you?' Isidora asked as she emptied the bowl of water into the channel and refilled it from the pipe in the wall. 'Did it have some special meaning?'

'It's just a phrase,' said Lucius. 'I'm sure I've heard him say it, but it never meant anything secret.'

At that moment there was a loud cheer from the arena. Lucius went out and saw the gladiators gathered around his uncle. Crassus was smiling widely. Quin was nearby, and when he saw Lucius he walked towards him. Lucius suddenly remembered that he needed to talk to his brother about Rufus. The message had knocked everything else out of his mind.

'What's going on?' he asked as Quin reached him.

'Our uncle is putting on a spectacle in honour of the new emperor,' said Quin. 'In a couple of weeks.'

He spoke stiffly, as if to a stranger. It made Lucius feel as if something was twisting in his chest.

'Who are the sponsors?' he asked.

'Just our uncle,' said Quin.

Lucius gaped at him. He had been hoping that a conversation about something new would clear the air. He hadn't expected this.

'*Ravilla* is paying for the whole spectacle?' he said slowly.

'That's what I just said.'

'But Quin... *how*?'

'What's the problem?' Quin asked. 'Why are you looking at me like that?'

112

'Like what?'

'Like you've found a bad smell.'

'Quin, I don't understand this. No – wait –' Lucius grabbed his brother's arm as he turned away. 'Listen! Father always said that Ravilla's money was spent on gambling and drinking. How has he suddenly got the money to pay for a spectacle?'

'Stop being so suspicious!' Quin snapped. 'Ravilla wants to honour Titus and show everyone a good time, and you just can't stand that he's a decent man.'

'But people have bankrupted themselves to pay for spectacles,' said Lucius. 'How has Ravilla got that sort of money?'

Quin looked as if he were going to explode. 'He's a senator and a nobleman, you idiot. He owns houses, collects rents from tenants – and besides which it's none of your business. I know why you're being so awkward. You don't want me to be a gladiator, but I am, and I'm going to fight in the spectacle, and there is *nothing* you can do about it. Right?'

Quin walked away and Lucius was left feeling even more confused. Quin wasn't even a tiro yet – could he really be ready in such a short time?

'Lucius, I've been thinking,' said Isidora behind him.

Lucius didn't reply. He was looking at Quin, who was now standing beside Ravilla, smiling broadly and laughing. Lucius knew that was for his benefit.

'Did you tell him about Rufus?' Isidora asked in a softer tone. 'Or the message?'

Lucius shook his head. 'He didn't give me the chance,' he said. 'And I don't think there would be any point anyway. He doesn't want to listen to anything I have to say any more.'

She squeezed his arm. It was a friendly gesture and he appreciated it.

'Listen,' she went on, 'you must have emptied your bag at the end of the day – when you delivered your last messages and came back to see if Crassus needed anything else?'

'Yes, but he was training – he just waved at me to go.'

'But how did you *know* that all your messages had been delivered?' she persisted. 'Did you check in your bag or did you just know how many messages there were?'

Lucius screwed up his eyes and tried to remember. He had looked into the bag many times over the course of the day – while crossing the Forum, while running through the streets – but when had been the last time? Then he opened his eyes.

'I remember!' he exclaimed, making Isidora jump. 'I checked inside the bag as I walked into the school – I remember because my hands were hot and tired, and it took me ages to undo the straps.'

Isidora's eyes flashed in excitement.

'So you walked into the school…'

'I walked into the school, and I leaned against one of the pillars and watched the training for a minute.'

114

'Did you notice anyone hanging around you – behind you?'

Her excitement was infectious – Lucius felt his heart beating faster.

'There were people hurrying around behind me – gladiators coming into the arena, slaves... I don't know who.'

'Anyone could have slipped the message into your bag as you were leaning against the pillar,' said Isidora. 'But it would have to have been someone who was in the school – and at that time of day the only people here were gladiators, doctores and slaves.'

'In other words,' said Lucius, 'if my father is back in Rome, he's in disguise and he's right here in the school.'

Lucius scrutinised the faces around him. Had his father somehow transformed himself into a humble slave or a novicius gladiator? He peered at the faces of the secutores, who were training closest to him.

Suddenly he felt a heavy hand on his shoulder. 'I have a job for you, boy,' Crassus said. 'The programmes are ready for Marcus Calidius's spectacle next week – I want you out selling them.'

Lucius longed to be able to refuse. The only thing he wanted to do was to check every person in the school in case one of them was his father. But only a fool would argue with Crassus, and a few minutes later he was walking out of the school, his bag stuffed with the programmes.

He glanced down at the programme in his hand. The list of gladiators who would be fighting seemed endless. Marcus Calidius, the sponsor who was paying for the spectacle, obviously wanted to impress the public. Ravilla's show, scheduled for the week after and with the emperor in attendance, would need to be even more impressive.

Lucius had never been to see the games. His father had not exactly forbidden it – Quin had been many times. But there was something about the look in Aquila's eyes when he talked about it that had made Lucius want to stay away to please him. Secretly he had wanted to see what Quin made such a fuss about, but the thought of the disappointed expression on his father's face was enough to deter him.

It didn't take him long to sell all the programmes – it was some time since the last spectacle and people were keen to enjoy themselves. Every time he went back to the school to get more programmes, Lucius checked his bag in case another message had appeared. He kept a lookout for anyone who walked close to him, but nothing strange happened.

The *Carpe diem* message had changed everything. He felt sure that his father was trying to contact him, and sooner or later he would succeed. Lucius was determined to be ready.

CHAPTER IX

ucius watched Ruga striding around the arena, holding himself very straight and tall. With his face covered by his angular helmet with feathers waving from the crest, he looked unbeatable. Lucius could see the heat shimmering off the metal. Some people in the crowd were already chanting his name.

From the opposite end of the arena, Lupus was loping towards Ruga in full Retiarius costume. Lucius shook his head. He had seen them laughing together, working together and training together. They were friends. But at this moment they looked as if they were implacable enemies. Quin had talked about the honesty of the arena – the straightforwardness of 'kill or be killed'. But it didn't seem very honest that friends had to act as if they hated each other.

Lucius was standing beside Quin at the far end of the temporary amphitheatre. Ravilla had said that he could attend the spectacle with his brother, and Quin seemed eager for Lucius to enjoy himself. After their last argument, Lucius had decided to avoid all subjects that might annoy his brother. He hadn't even said anything about Rufus, knowing that his brother would criticise his 'suspicious nature'. As a result, Quin had been positively friendly. He had taken it upon himself to educate Lucius in the ways of the arena.

'You see how Lupus has his manica* on his left arm?' he said. 'That's one of the things that makes Retiarii different – it makes it easier to use the net.'

'What's that on his galerus?' Lucius asked, squinting in an effort to see the engraving on Lupus's shoulder protector.

'He has sea creatures – crabs and dolphins, that kind of thing,' said Quin. 'I wouldn't want that on mine. I want something really heroic – maybe an image of Hercules, or my weapons.'

Lucius didn't trust himself to be able to sound genuinely enthusiastic about this, so he said nothing. Besides, it was getting harder to hear a word his brother said. The crowd was working itself up into a noisy frenzy, desperate to see the fight.

* manica: a sleeve-like arm guard made of metal strips backed with leather. Retiarii wore a manica and a galerus (shoulder guard) on the left arm only.

When they were no more than an arm's length apart, the gladiators turned to face the podium where Marcus Calidius was sitting. He waved them on graciously.

Ruga and Lupus started to circle each other. Lucius folded his arms and tucked his clenched fists into his armpits. He didn't want to watch, and yet it was fascinating to see them pretend to size each other up. They had known each other for years – they knew exactly what their strengths and weaknesses were. But the crowd wanted to see it, and Crassus made sure they got what they wanted.

Lupus walked backwards as Ruga came slowly towards him. The roar of the crowd grew louder and more passionate. They wanted blood. Lupus jabbed his trident towards Ruga, who lurched to one side and nearly lost his footing.

The crowd was screaming now, and Lupus was laughing, still stabbing his trident at Ruga. Lupus threw his net so quickly that Lucius didn't even see it fly through the air – but Ruga was a match for him. He turned so that the net caught on his gladius* rather than his shield.

Lupus pulled on the net, using all his strength to draw Ruga towards the prongs of his trident. The crowd went wild – were they about to see first blood? Ruga dragged his gladius through the net, cutting it,

* *gladius: a Roman infantry sword. 'Gladiator' means 'a person who fights with the gladius'.*

and Lupus quickly flicked it free – neither of them wanted to lose their weapons this early.

The battle increased in speed and intensity. First Ruga and then Lupus would attack and be knocked back. Time and time again the net flicked through the air; the gladius tried to jab past the trident. They were both sweating freely now, the raging sun making their bare chests gleam.

Again they circled each other.

'Lupus is doing well,' said Quin. 'He's keeping Ruga at trident's length – that gives him the advantage.'

Lucius didn't reply. His mouth felt dry. Suddenly the trident jabbed dangerously close to Ruga's chest, but this time it met his shield. The sound of metal on leather-clad wood could not be heard above the shouts of the crowd, but everyone heard Ruga's roar of attack as his gladius smashed down on Lupus's trident, knocking it from his hand. Lupus ran and Ruga followed him, being careful to stand between his opponent and the trident.

The crowd cheered Lupus as he ran, with Ruga lumbering after him.

'He's got to tire Ruga out,' Quin said, leaning forward as if he wished he could run out there. 'Look how light he is on his feet!'

Lupus led Ruga around the arena twice before the Murmillo slowed his pace, his shoulders rolling forwards and his knees shaking as he battled for breath. Lupus saw his chance and sprinted towards his trident, which was still lying in the centre of the arena. Ruga saw him and found his strength again. He charged towards Lupus like a wild beast, but at the last moment Lupus hurled his net and entangled Ruga's head and sword arm.

Ruga held his shield in front of him, trying to drag the net from his head.

'He can't see!' Quin cried in excitement. '*Now*, Lupus!'

Lupus kicked Ruga's legs from under him and the Murmillo crashed to the ground, his shield flying out of his grasp.

Someone in the crowd started a chant of 'Kill! Kill! Kill!', which was quickly taken up by the masses. Lupus stood over him and slowly lowered his short sword to Ruga's neck. He had won.

Lupus lifted his sword and Ruga rolled over and pulled himself up onto his knees. He placed one hand on Lupus's thigh in the usual way, and then all eyes turned to Marcus Calidius.

The sponsor was leaning forward just like Quin, his eyes bright. The chant of the crowd was deafening now: 'Kill! Kill! Kill!'

Marcus Calidius put out his hand and held it steady. Lucius started to relax. The sponsor would have to pay out a lot of money for the death of the primus palus – and he had already spent a fortune on the spectacle. He was sure to indicate life for the Murmillo by covering his thumb.

There was a gasp all around the amphitheatre as Marcus Calidius clearly stretched his thumb out to the side. Death!

'A generous sponsor,' said Bestia from behind Lucius. 'Now there's a rare beast.'

The crowd cheered his generosity – they knew how much he would have to pay to give them the blood they wanted. Lucius thought he saw Lupus's lips move – had he said something to Ruga? Then his short sword plunged into Ruga's neck, and the entire amphitheatre erupted with cheers, roars and shouts.

Lucius felt numb as he watched Lupus take the victory palm and jog around the arena, spattered in vivid sprays of Ruga's blood. The attendants entered the arena, dressed as Charon and Mercury,* to check Ruga was dead and remove his body.

Lupus approached Marcus Calidius to receive his prize. Lucius, whose feet had been rooted to the spot, turned away. His stomach was churning.

'What's the matter?' Quin asked. 'You've gone quite white.'

'Doesn't it bother you?' Lucius asked, feeling more miserable than surprised. 'You've trained with that man. He said you would make a good gladiator. Doesn't his death affect you?'

'Lucius, if you can't handle the raw truth of the arena then you should go home and ask Mother to

* *Charon: Romans believed that he ferried dead souls across the River Styx to the land of the dead. Mercury: the god who served as messenger to the gods.*

teach you to spin,' said Quin. 'We get *taught* how to die with honour. It's part of the game. To see Ruga die like that – with such courage – it's inspiring.'

Lucius suddenly longed to punch his brother in the mouth. He had to get away.

'I forgot something at the school,' he said, pushing his way past the gladiators behind him. The sweat from their bare chests smeared his tunic as he passed.

'Wait!' Quin shouted. '*What* did you forget? Come back!' But his voice was already lost amid the roars of the crowd – the next match was about to start. Lucius pelted away, glad that the streets were not as crowded as usual. He didn't want to hear any more of the bloodthirsty chanting.

Lucius didn't stop until he was back inside the school, his throat burning and his chest tight. He drank some water from the nearest fountain and closed his eyes. Instantly he saw Ruga on his knees and the sword flashing down. His eyes blinked open wide again and he took a few deep breaths.

With no gladiators training in the arena, the school seemed very quiet. Some of the slaves had been given leave to go and watch the games, and the others would be preparing for the return of the gladiators. What would happen to Ruga's room? Isidora always complained about having to clean it because of the number of victory palms he had in there.

There was a muffled bang from the direction of Ravilla's study, and Lucius looked around in surprise.

The room was only ever used by Ravilla, and he would be at the spectacle. Surely no slave would be cleaning at this time of day?

His calcei scrunched softly on the sand as he walked across the arena towards the offices. The hairs on his arms stood up – his skin was prickling again. The sunlight was so bright that when he stepped between the pillars into the shaded corridor, he could hardly see a thing. He reached out and held on to the side of the doorway, blinking to accustom his eyes to the shade. He could hear a faint noise, like the rustle of papyrus. Someone was inside the room.

Lucius took one step into the room and nearly jumped out of his skin as Rufus loomed towards him out of the shadows.

'What are you doing in here?' he asked, wincing as his voice squeaked. He didn't want to sound scared. Rufus merely stepped past him and walked out. Lucius whirled around, his fear dispersed by his outrage.

'You can't just ignore my questions!' he shouted at Rufus's disappearing back. 'This is my uncle's room! Why aren't you at the spectacle?'

Rufus's long strides had already taken him to the entrance. Seconds later, various surprised-looking slaves appeared from the rooms around the arena.

'Lucius!' called Isidora, who was standing in the kitchen doorway. 'What on earth are you shouting about?'

Lucius held out his arm after Rufus, who had now completely disappeared from sight.

'He… he was…'

His anger seemed to have rendered him unable to speak.

'Been in the sun too long,' Secundus grunted. 'Have some water and get on with your work.'

As the others went back to their duties, Isidora slipped along the corridor towards Lucius.

'What's wrong?' she asked.

'Rufus!' Lucius erupted. 'He was in there, snooping!'

'In your uncle's study?' asked Isidora, looking astonished. 'Why? There's nothing in there.' She peered into the room and shrugged. 'Just a few scrolls.'

'I don't trust that man,' Lucius said. 'He's up to something.'

Isidora gave him a look that he didn't understand.

'Lucius…' she began, and then paused.

'What?' he demanded. 'Isidora, do you know something about Rufus?'

'Lucius, he's just a slave,' she said. 'What can he do? Even if he was trying to find something in there, he won't have succeeded. I don't think you should be worrying about *him*.'

'What does that mean?' Lucius felt as if he were going to explode. 'Why do I always feel as if no one tells me anything?'

She looked very uneasy now. When she spoke again, her voice was low and measured.

'I think that the person you should be worrying about is your uncle,' she said.

Lucius felt as if his eyebrows were knotting themselves together.

'What are you talking about?'

'Come in here.' She pulled him into the study and lowered her voice even further. 'Lucius, I lived with your uncle for eleven years, and I know him. I know his expressions. I know how he does things.'

Her soft whisper and the gleam of her eyes in the shadows made a shiver ripple down Lucius's spine.

'So…?'

'So… he's been paying a lot of attention to Quin lately,' she went on. 'More than before. I see them walking and talking together, and I see the look in his eyes, and it scares me.'

'What look?' Lucius asked. 'I don't understand.'

'It's a sort of cunning, sly look,' she said. 'I don't know how to explain it.'

But she didn't need to. In trying to describe it, she had, for a moment, reproduced the look on her own face. In that instant Lucius recognised it and knew that he had seen it too.

'I know what you mean,' he said quickly. 'But that's just Ravilla – he's always had a bit of a sly look about him.'

'Lucius, when I lived with him I was often in the room when he was talking business to other men,' she said. 'And when I saw him look at a man like that,

I knew what to expect. A few days or weeks later, I'd hear that man had lost all his money, or fallen out with some important person, or... or been unlucky in some way.'

Lucius felt his stomach turn over. If anyone heard Isidora talking that way, she would be beaten. He shouldn't be allowing a slave girl to talk about his kinsman like this. But there was no one to whom he could turn.

'He's my uncle,' he said, knowing how feeble it sounded. 'He wouldn't do us any harm.'

Even as he spoke, he could hear his father's voice in an unguarded moment. 'Ravilla would take a beggar's last crumb if he thought there was profit in it.'

'I've got an idea,' said Isidora. 'Do you know about the room your uncle keeps here?'

'This one?'

'No, there's another one below the barracks,' she said, still whispering. 'We're not supposed to clean it. Secundus told me that it's a place for him to work and think in peace.'

This was very strange news.

'But he has his own villa,' Lucius said, trying and failing to force sense out of the strangeness. 'He has no wife or children demanding his attention. It's probably more peaceful there than here.'

'Exactly,' said Isidora. 'So what does he do there?' Lucius felt excitement and fear mingling in his blood.

'What are you suggesting?' he asked, already knowing the answer.

'Break in,' she replied swiftly. 'If there's something going on that you need to know about, I'm sure you'll find out about it in there.'

He realised that he had already made the decision to do it. He nodded and took a deep breath.

'All right,' he said. 'Tell me where it is and then go back to the kitchens. I'll be as fast as I can.'

Isidora put her hands on her hips and looked belligerent.

'I don't think so, aristo boy,' she said. 'You're not leaving me out of this – it's my idea!'

Lucius shook his head.

'If you get caught, you'll get beaten,' he said. 'This is my problem and I'm not putting you in danger for it.'

'Don't be stupid,' said Isidora, looking very irritable. 'For one thing you don't even know where the room is, and I'm not telling you if you leave me behind. And for another thing you'll need me to be a lookout in case anyone comes.'

'No, it's not fair on you.'

'I'll be the judge of that, thank you.'

Lucius drew himself up very tall. 'Isidora, I order you to tell me where that room is and then go to the kitchens.'

The annoying girl just laughed at him. 'No, aristo boy, and you're wasting time by arguing. Almost everyone is watching the spectacle – there will never be a better chance than this.'

He glared at her, but he could see that she was going to be very stubborn about this.

'All right,' he said eventually. 'But I'm not happy about it.'

'That *is* going to keep me awake at night,' she said with a grin. 'Come on!'

CHAPTER X

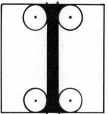sidora led Lucius over to the east side of the arena, where the steps led up to Crassus's quarters. A narrower set of stairs led downwards into blackness.

'I thought only the slave prison was down there,' said Lucius.

'That's what most people think,' she replied. 'I only found Ravilla's room because I was being too keen and looking for something to clean. Secundus wasn't happy.'

She took a step downwards, then gave an exclamation and darted away. Lucius watched her vanish into the kitchen, wondering what had suddenly occurred to her. A couple of minutes passed, and then she came back holding a lighted lucerna.*

* *lucerna: a Roman lamp, usually made of pottery, shaped like a bowl with a handle on one side and a spout on the other.*

'It would help if we could see,' she said, as she reached him.

'Good thinking,' he replied.

She led the way down the narrow steps. A stale, musty smell wafted up towards them and Lucius wrinkled his nose.

'I wouldn't choose to work down there,' he said.

'You would if it was something that you wanted to hide from the authorities,' Isidora pointed out.

'My father always said that if there was anything underhand going on, Ravilla would surely know something about it,' said Lucius.

Isidora laughed. 'He would do more than just know about it,' she said. 'He would be in the middle of it, right up to his neck.'

They had reached the foot of the steps and were now walking along a narrow corridor. The stink of urine stung Lucius's eyes and burned the back of his throat. All was blackness apart from the glow of light from the lucerna in Isidora's hand. It made her long braid gleam purplish-black in front of him.

'When I lived in his villa, visitors would come at all hours of the day and night,' she said. 'We were told to be deaf and blind to anything we saw or heard. If we failed, our punishment was… harsh.'

The last word reverberated with meaning. Lucius said nothing. Strangely, in the darkness he felt as if he could see her more clearly. She felt things more deeply than he had realised. He wanted to ask about her parents, but he didn't want to upset her.

'What happened to…' he began, and then hesitated, feeling clumsy.

'A lot of slaves die in Ravilla's service,' said Isidora, a tremor creeping into her voice. 'Sometimes they die from simple illnesses because they are not treated. But it isn't healthy for them to have too much knowledge. His slaves seem to be very *accident-prone*.'

'Isidora…'

Lucius understood exactly what she was saying, and he felt horribly unhappy.

'Either way,' she said, sounding normal again, 'he is guilty of a lot worse than just telling a few lies to your mother. So let's find out what. Here's the door.'

She stopped in front of a heavy wooden door and held up the lucerna. The warm yellow light fell on a sturdy-looking lock.

'I should have guessed,' said Lucius, disappointment crashing down upon him. 'It's no good. We can't break in because then he'll know someone's been here.'

'True,' said Isidora, turning to look at him with a mischievous glint in her eyes. 'It's just as well I've got this then, isn't it?'

Lucius gaped at her as she held up a bronze key.

'When I went to get the lucerna, the kitchen was empty,' she said. 'I slipped through to Secundus's side room, where he keeps all the keys, and he wasn't there. So I thought I would just borrow this!'

133

Lucius shook his head. Her impulsiveness was wonderful and terrifying – Secundus could notice that the key was missing at any moment.

'Open it up, quickly,' he said. 'We haven't got much time.'

She turned the key in the lock and Lucius heard the bolt squeak open. Isidora opened the door and they stepped inside.

The table and chair in the centre virtually filled the whole room. Lucius had to press his back against the wall to fit inside. He edged his way around to the chair and sat down. There were three leather boxes on the table. As silently as a shadow, Isidora put the lucerna on the table and slipped out of the door to listen for anyone coming.

One by one, Lucius opened the leather boxes on the table. The first two were empty. When Lucius came to the last one he had almost lost hope, but to his delight he found a single wax tablet. He laid it down on the table and pulled the lucerna closer. Now he could see columns and the adding and subtracting of amounts of money. There was nothing to say where the money was from or where it was going.

'Isidora!' Lucius said in a loud whisper. 'Come and look at this.'

She was back in an instant, and poring over the figures.

'He's balancing finances,' said Lucius.

'Money in and money out,' she agreed. 'But what a *lot* of money!'

She was right. If this was a record of Ravilla's income, it explained how he could afford to put on a spectacle. What it didn't explain was where the money was coming from.

'Ravilla's a borrower, not a lender,' said Lucius. 'But if this were a record of what he had borrowed, surely he would have listed the lenders' names? And this third column is the balance – it looks as if all this money belongs to him.'

He shook his head in confusion, and put the wax tablet back.

'Aren't you going to take it?' Isidora asked.

'And let him know that someone has been snooping?' said Lucius. 'Not a good idea. Besides, what do these figures prove? I came here to find out if he's planning something for Quin, not to investigate his income.'

He picked up the lucerna and held it high above his head. It eerily illuminated the room, making strangely shaped patterns on the black walls. Lucius guessed that it was probably a solitary cell, designed to harrow up the souls of unfortunate slaves. He thought again what a peculiar place his uncle had chosen as a workroom.

'There's nothing else in here,' he said. 'Let's go back upstairs and return the key before Secundus starts thundering.'

They left the room and Isidora carefully turned the key in the lock. Then she led him back along the corridor. It seemed to take longer this time. He thought that he glimpsed the light at the foot of the steps, but then it disappeared. He was about to ask if she had taken a wrong turn when the lucerna tumbled to the ground and went out. Lucius heard Isidora gasp and give a little cry of fear. Then he saw a dark shape moving in front of her, like a living shadow. It was this that was blocking out the light.

Lucius reached for Isidora in the darkness and dragged her back towards him. Apart from her first cry she was silent, but as he pushed her behind him he could feel her trembling.

'Who are you?' he demanded. 'Name yourself.'

He heard a scratch and a hiss, and then a pungent smell met his nostrils as a sulphur match ignited in front of him. It illuminated a pale face and a thatch of red hair.

'Rufus!' he said.

'Get out of here,' said the new novicius.

His lips barely moved when he spoke.

'You can't tell us —'

'Get out of here and don't come back,' said Rufus. 'If you know what's good for you.'

He stood aside and Lucius saw the light streaming down the steps at the end of the corridor. Conscious that they had to return the key, he bent down to retrieve the lucerna and then pulled Isidora along with him. He didn't turn around, but he knew that Rufus was watching. The man's eyes were boring into his back.

CHAPTER XI

ne, then two, then three days passed, and still nothing had come of their adventure underground. The key had apparently not been missed. But Lucius could not relax. He felt as if his sinews were tight to the point of snapping, and the slightest unexpected noise made him jump. Even at home he felt nervous and uneasy. He slept badly, and he started yawning long before Valeria's bedtime.

'Lazybones,' his sister said, prodding her finger into his ribs. 'Want to play a game?'

'Val, I'm too tired. And I'm surprised you aren't too, working all day in that shack.'

'Today was fun!' said Valeria. 'We were polishing swords and helmets. Then this giant gladiator came in, Africanus. He said they were the shiniest weapons and armour he'd ever seen. Oh, *please* play a game, Luicus.'

'Play a game with Mother.'

They both looked across at their mother, who was leaning back on the couch, her spindle untouched in front of her.

'She's thinking again,' said Valeria. 'She thinks a lot nowadays, doesn't she.'

Lucius was of the opinion that thinking was the exact opposite of what his mother was doing, but he said nothing. He didn't know how to explain it to himself, let alone to Valeria.

'All right,' he said, giving his head a shake to try to loosen some extra mental energy. 'One game. What will you choose?'

'Twelve Lines?' she said at once.

'All right – get the board.'

Suddenly a loud squeak told them that someone was coming up the stairs. Before Lucius knew it he was on his feet, fists clenched.

'Calm down, silly!' Valeria said with a laugh. 'It's only Quin!'

Their brother's head peered around the door, grinning at them. Valeria ran to him and he lifted her into the air and spun her around.

'Put me down!' she cried, giggling helplessly.

'Quin!' said Caecilia, rising to her feet and moving towards him with her hands held out.

Quin put Valeria down and took his mother's hands. 'We've missed you,' she said.

It was the first time he had been home in weeks. He looked at Lucius and laughed.

'You're getting nervous, little brother,' he said. 'You look skinny. We need to make you look more like a man and less like a scared rat.'

Lucius didn't laugh. He was getting used to the sudden waves of anger that came over him these days. It made his insides writhe to see his mother and sister smiling and laughing just because Quin had been gracious enough to show his face. And yet hadn't he once adored Quin just as much as they did? It wasn't so very long ago that he had hung on his brother's every word, but it seemed a lifetime away.

'Are you staying here tonight?' Valeria asked. 'Please say yes!'

'Sorry, Val, not tonight,' he replied. 'I only came to give you some news – I wanted to tell you myself.'

He was radiant with it, whatever it was. Caecilia led him to her couch and sat beside him. Valeria leaned against his other arm. Lucius sat down slowly, facing them.

'Crassus – the Doctor Retiarius – took me aside this evening and told me that my initial training is complete,' he said. 'I'm officially a tiro.'

Caecilia's hand drifted upwards to cover her mouth.

'What does it mean?' Valeria asked.

139

'It means that I'm ready to fight in public combat,' said Quin. 'As soon as I've done that, I'll be a veteranus. I'll have my own quarters at the school, instead of sleeping in the barracks. I'll be a proper gladiator!'

He looked so happy that part of Lucius longed to be able to congratulate him. But the words stuck in his throat. It was all happening much too fast.

'I bet you'll be the best gladiator,' said Valeria.

'It means I can start earning purses,' Quin went on. 'I can give you some money, Mother. Life will get easier from now on.'

Caecilia rubbed his arm and smiled. Quin looked at her with a sudden gleam of surprise in his eyes.

'You're not going to tell me to be careful?' he asked. 'Or tell me that you don't want me to get hurt?'

'I'm sure that you know the best thing to do,' she said.

Quin's smile faded a little and he glanced at Lucius.

'*Are* you going to get hurt?' asked Valeria in a small voice.

'No, of course not,' said Quin, giving her a squeeze.

'Do they teach you how to lie as well as how to die?' Lucius asked.

He felt bad as soon as he had said it, but he didn't seem able to stop himself.

'What is that supposed to mean?' Quin growled.

'It's all a great big mesh of lies,' Lucius said. 'Now you're lying to your own family.'

'What does he mean?' Valeria asked, her voice rising higher.

'Nothing,' said Quin.

'Tell her,' Lucius persisted. 'Yes, you'll get a nice fat purse of money if you win. And if you lose then *maybe* you'll get away with a few wounds where a sword has sliced through your flesh. Or maybe the stupid crowd will decide that they've had enough of your face, or they don't like the pattern on your galerus, and then you'll be kneeling on the ground waiting to feel the sword jab through your throat!'

Quin had risen from the couch as Lucius was talking. He walked forward, grabbed Lucius by the arm and pulled him outside and down the stairs into the street without even breaking his stride. It happened so fast that Lucius was still talking when he hit the ground. Quin stood over him, taking long, deep breaths as if to steady himself.

'I'm trying very hard not to hit you,' he said. 'So stop talking.'

Lucius sat up, brushing the dust off his tunic and leaning back against the wall of the fast-food shop. The shock of landing on his back seemed to have stopped the dreadful writhing feeling in his chest.

'It's not fair to say things like that to Valeria,' Quin went on. 'What good does it do? Who is it going to help?'

'It's the truth,' said Lucius. 'I believe in telling the truth. I don't understand why it's so hard.' But he

141

could hear his sister crying from inside the house, and he knew that he wasn't going to win this debate.

'All I'm asking you to do is to avoid telling them things that will hurt them,' Quin said. 'Is that really so bad? Now, what's going on? Is Mother ill?'

Lucius shook his head. The tiredness swept over him again, and he felt his head drooping.

'She's been like that for weeks,' he murmured. 'It's as if she's not really here most of the time.'

Quin turned and started to walk around in a small circle, staring at the ground.

'I can't be here *and* focus on my training,' he said. 'I need you to make sure that Mother and Val are all right. Learning to be a gladiator is my job. Looking after things at home is yours.'

'But that was *your* choice,' said Lucius. 'You never even asked me.'

'Lucius, you're getting it all wrong,' said Quin. 'It wasn't *my* choice or your choice or anyone's choice except Aquila's. *He* betrayed us all. *He* put us in this position. And now Mother is like a stranger, and that's his doing too.'

Lucius rubbed his forehead. Quin's logic sounded simple, but it didn't take into account any of the subtleties and questions he knew existed.

Lucius wanted to make Quin sit down and listen. He wanted to explain all the things that had made him worried and suspicious, but he was so tired that everything was muddled in his mind. Besides, even if he had been able to link all his thoughts together, he wasn't sure that Quin would understand. He loved his brother, but he knew now that they had different ways of looking at things.

'I'm too tired,' he said.

Quin held out a hand, and Lucius grabbed it and let his brother pull him up.

'I have to go back to the school now,' said Quin. 'They're doing my tattoos in the morning.'

'Not on your face?' said Lucius, hating the thought of the brand.

'Legs and arms, I think,' said Quin, smiling at him. 'It's all right, you know. We all have them.'

'Do you know when you're going to be fighting?'

'Ravilla wants me in his spectacle,' said Quin.

'Do you think the Emperor will come?'

Quin shrugged. 'We'll see.'

He embraced Lucius, and then set off back to the school. Lucius watched him go, his upright frame getting smaller and smaller, until he vanished around a corner.

In the distance, Lucius heard the whine of a dog, and it made him think wistfully of Argos. How he would have loved to cuddle his big old dog right now.

'Where's Quin?' Valeria asked as soon as he went back inside.

'He had to go back.'

'You sent him away!' Valeria shouted. 'Why did you do that? Why did you say all those horrible things?'

143

'Val, I—'

'Leave me alone!' she said, shaking his hand off her arm. 'I'm going to bed!'

Lucius longed for his bed too. He bent down and kissed his mother's cheek.

'Good night,' he said. 'I'm sorry.'

'You mustn't argue with your brother,' she murmured. 'You boys.'

Lucius went to his room and lay down fully clothed. The shutters were still open, and the cool night breeze wafted over him. For the first time since his encounter with Rufus, he felt peaceful. It was as if shouting at Quin had released something. At that moment, he wasn't sure that he would ever have the strength to feel angry again.

Thoughts of Quin, Ravilla and Rufus floated through his mind like cobwebs on the wind, getting tangled up with his questions about his father, Ravilla's hidden finances and the mysterious message. He started to dream, and in his dream the cobwebs drew together, forming one vast web that blocked him every way he turned, trapping him like a fly. He could not get away, and he knew that there must be a spider close by, watching him and waiting for its moment.

The day before the start of Ravilla's spectacle, Lucius was keeping himself as busy as he could to avoid thinking about what might happen. It still felt strange to see Quin training with real weapons, in full armour. Lucius had tried to imagine what it would be like to watch his brother in the arena, but it seemed as if he were just dressing up.

'He looks good, doesn't he?' Lucius asked Isidora as they were preparing food. 'I mean, he's handling the weapons well.'

They could see the gladiators hard at work in the training arena. The Retiarii were practising with their nets – taking it in turns to fling them over each other. Quin hadn't missed his mark once. Isidora gave a loud sniff.

'Perhaps he should try throwing his net over that Britannic hulk,' she said. 'He's always watching him.'

She was still seething about the fact that Rufus had managed to scare her. Lucius suspected that she was as fierce an enemy as she was a friend. For a moment he almost pitied Rufus.

'He never even changes his expression, have you noticed?' she went on. 'Always that horrible, blank look. Did you ever remember where you had seen him before, by the way?'

Lucius shook his head. 'I'm not sure any more,' he said. 'Maybe I saw him for sale one day or something.'

'I still think you ought to tell Quin about him,' she said.

'Isidora, Quin wouldn't understand why I was worrying,' he replied. 'He deals in facts. If I told him that Rufus stares at him, he'd probably just think he was studying his technique. You know that Rufus has been made a tiro as well – they might have to fight each other.'

'And what about going through his things?'

'He'd say it was probably just a mistake,' Lucius told her. 'Who knows, maybe he'd be right.'

'Are you being annoying on purpose?' Isidora demanded. 'Don't tell me that searching your uncle's room and following us underground and refusing to answer questions is innocent.'

'All right, I agree with you,' said Lucius with a laugh. 'But we can't do anything without proof.'

He picked up a couple of water jugs and went to fill them from the nearest fountain.

'Lucius, when you've done that you can take the final amphitheatre arrangements to Donatus,' Crassus yelled. 'I've put them in your bag in Ravilla's office.'

Lucius nodded without meeting Crassus's eye. The mention of Ravilla's office brought back the memory of that horrible little room underground, and he felt as if his guilt must be printed on his face. He filled the jugs, put them in the mess hall and then went to pick up his bag.

The wax tablet was sitting on top of the scroll containing the amphitheatre plans. Lucius stared at it in shock, hardly able to believe his eyes. The handwriting was unmistakeable.

He snatched up the message and read it hungrily. 'Aventine, sunset. You know where. Come alone. Tell no one.'

Lucius made an instant decision not to tell Isidora. She might want to go with him, and besides, his father had asked him to say nothing. He felt absolutely sure that this message had come from his father. They had once visited the Aventine wool market together, and close to Porta Naevia they had found a little cluster of trees around a small clearing. It had provided a quiet haven from the bustle of the market in the neighbouring field; that must be the place his father was referring to.

'What are you dawdling in here for?' grumbled Secundus from the doorway. 'Didn't I just hear Crassus give you an order?'

Lucius slipped the wax tablet into his bag as casually as he could, trying to make it look as if it were nothing important. He felt as if Secundus must be able to hear his heart thumping from across the room. But the chief slave merely grunted disapprovingly at him and walked on. Happiness, relief and excitement were jostling for a place in Lucius's heart. Tonight he would see his father. Tonight everything would be explained at last. And perhaps, by some miracle, Aquila would find a way to take Quin out of the school before the spectacle – before he had to risk his life.

Time seemed to stretch and the hours passed impossibly slowly. It seemed as if evening would never come. But finally the last message of the day was delivered, the last duty was performed, and Crassus said that Lucius could go.

It took longer than he expected to walk south to the Aventine, and longer still to make his way along the city wall until he reached Porta Naevia. His feet were aching after another day of running messages, but the nearer he drew to the clearing, the less he noticed the pain in his heels. He burst into the clearing just as the sun sank behind him.

'Father!' he called out, desperate now to hear Aquila's steady tones, his answering voice saying Lucius's name.

But the little clearing was empty and silent. There wasn't so much as an echo to answer him.

CHAPTER XII

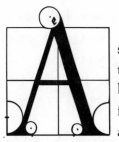s soon as Lucius reached the school the following morning, he found it buzzing with preparations for the first fights that afternoon. Not far away, in the temporary wooden amphitheatre, the animals were already tearing each other apart. It would be the turn of the human warriors after lunch.

Lucius was kept busy running messages and instructions between the school and the amphitheatre, and he was glad of the distraction. The thought of what had happened – or rather, failed to happen – the previous evening was hard to ignore. He could forget about it briefly while he was on an errand, and he would have a few minutes of relief. Then it would come back to him, like someone whispering poisonous words in his ear.

He had waited until long past sunset. At one point he had thought that he heard someone coming, but it must have been some small animal rustling through the undergrowth, because no one had appeared.

Why hadn't his father come? Had he had an accident? It couldn't have been a trick – no one else knew about the little clearing they had found together. Lucius was half expecting to hear that his father had been seen and arrested, but the morning wore on and no such news reached his ears.

He was scrubbing the tables in the mess hall when his brother found him. The look on Quin's face showed that he was in a state of indignant rage.

'I've been here longer than Rufus,' he declared, banging his fist down on one of the tables. 'Why aren't I a tiro? It's not fair.'

Quin had hoped that he would be one of the first to fight, but he wasn't scheduled to appear until the second day of the spectacle. However, Rufus was to battle a Hoplomachus* called Pulcher that afternoon, and Quin was incensed by the fact that Rufus would become a veteranus sooner than him.

'He'll want to be primus palus next, just you wait and see,' he grumbled.

'That's ridiculous,' Lucius said, moving on to the

---

* *Hoplomachus: a gladiator equipped as a hoplite (a heavily armed Greek infantryman). Pulcher's name means 'handsome'.*

next table. 'He won't be made primus palus after one match.'

'Well I wouldn't have thought he'd make tiro after a few weeks,' his brother retorted. 'But it happened.'

'What is it that you don't like about him?' asked Lucius, wondering how much Quin had noticed.

'No one likes him,' was the reply. 'He isn't interested in being part of the familia – he's too proud.'

'Don't you think there's something a bit… *strange* about him?' Lucius went on, wondering whether to tell Quin some of his suspicions after all. 'Did Ravilla – I mean – who found him?'

'I have no idea, but I hope they never prosper,' Quin snapped. 'The doctores think he's a gift from the gods.'

Lucius finished his scrubbing and grabbed the bucket full of dirty water.

'I have to go,' he said. 'Look, don't worry about Rufus. Just concentrate on being ready for your fight tomorrow. You won't care what Rufus is doing when you're in the middle of that arena.'

He hadn't seen Isidora so far that morning, but as he crossed the arena to the kitchen she was coming down the steps from Crassus's quarters.

'Aren't you going to watch the spectacle?' she asked with a mischievous smile.

'I can live without seeing a pack of wild animals rip holes in each other,' he replied.

'Are you talking about the beasts or the gladiators?'

He smiled and carried on walking. She fell into step beside him.

'Are you going to watch Quin's match tomorrow?' she asked.

'I don't want to,' he replied. 'I know he's expecting it, but it was bad enough seeing Ruga…'

'You don't think they'd call for death, do you?' she said in surprise. 'Not on his first match.'

'I suppose not, but I'm still not keen on seeing him hurt.'

'Maybe he won't be hurt,' she said. 'Maybe he'll win.'

'He's fighting an experienced Secutor, Isidora.'

'Experienced doesn't always mean better,' she replied. 'Although…'

He looked at her sharply. 'Although what?'

'It's just that some of the slaves were talking last night – who would they put a bet on if they had the money, you know. And they were all saying that they think Rufus must have been a gladiator before.'

'But that's impossible,' said Lucius. 'He'd have tattoos – he'd have a reputation.'

'I know,' she replied. 'But they think he's too good to be completely new at this.' Lucius frowned; here was yet another reason to be suspicious of Rufus, and yet he still had nothing definite to say against him.

'Lucius!' said Secundus, emerging from the kitchen like a stone from a sling. 'I have a job for you. The dormitories still haven't been cleaned and Crassus has taken half the slaves with him to the amphitheatre.'

Lucius nodded and went to fetch the sawdust and a broom. He liked Secundus, who was a kind man underneath his roars and orders. Besides, he was glad to have jobs that allowed him to be alone. His head felt ready to explode.

It was lunchtime and the dormitories were empty now – the gladiators were either training in the arena or gathering to go to the amphitheatre. Lucius shook the sawdust over the floor, put down the bucket and then nearly jumped out of his skin. Rufus was filling the doorway, staring silently at him.

'How long have you been there?' Lucius asked.

He didn't expect a reply and he didn't receive one. Gritting his teeth, he started to sweep out the farthest corner of the dormitory. He deliberately turned his back to the door, hoping that the man would leave. But, when he turned around, Rufus was standing a few steps behind him. Lucius stepped back, suddenly conscious of how big Rufus was, and what an inadequate weapon a broom would be.

'What do you want?' he asked. 'Either open your mouth and speak to me or leave me alone.'

His words were bold, but his voice sounded feeble to his own ears. He could hear a faint buzzing in his ears, and his trembling hand was making the broom handle shake. He pressed it against his body and tried to decide if he should make a run for it.

Rufus kept his gaze fixed on Lucius's eyes, but he reached out a hand to his own bag, which was lying on a bench beside him. His expression didn't change as he reached inside the bag. Lucius cleared his throat. Time stretched out as the pale hand emerged from the bag and held something out towards him.

Lucius stared at the small object that Rufus was holding up. It didn't make sense, and his mind seemed to be refusing to work properly. Very slowly he reached out his hand and took the ring from between Rufus's fingers.

'This... this belongs to my father,' he said.

Rufus gave one slow nod. Lucius gazed down at the ring. It had belonged on his father's little finger for as long as he could remember.

'Did you steal it from him?' he asked.

This time Rufus gave his head a slow shake. He beckoned to Lucius and walked to the side of the room that was farthest from the doorway. Lucius followed him, clutching the ring in his palm so hard that it dug into his skin.

'Tell me how you came by this,' he demanded.

'Your father is my master,' Rufus stated.

'No he's not,' said Lucius at once. 'I knew all his slaves – you were never in the villa. I never saw you.'

'Yes, indeed,' Rufus replied. 'You saw me once, many years ago when you were a small boy. We played ball in the garden while your father prepared some scrolls for me to carry.'

Lucius closed his eyes. Could he remember that day? Sunshine beating down on a red-gold thatch of hair… or was his imagination just filling in a memory?

'I don't believe you,' he said. 'Father's slaves came and went many times a day – you were never there.'

'Your father is a wise man,' Rufus said, unruffled. 'Sometimes discretion is required. Long journeys may be necessary. It is not always useful for people to know who you serve.'

Lucius frowned. 'You're telling me that you're some sort of secret slave? Why would Father need such a thing? It doesn't make sense.'

'Powerful men make powerful enemies,' Rufus said. 'It was important for your father to have someone he could trust.'

'He trusted *you*?'

Lucius knew that he sounded rude and doubtful, but he had stopped worrying what Rufus might do to him. All he cared about was finding the truth.

'Without trust, we would have nothing,' said Rufus.

'Stop talking in riddles!' Lucius yelled, flinging the broom to the ground. 'I'm sick of feeling as if everyone knows something I don't! Just tell me what's going on! I want the truth!'

His words seemed to bounce off the walls, and for the first time he detected a flicker of amusement in Rufus's eyes. The gladiator sat down and placed his hands on his knees.

155

'When I was younger than you are now, I was standing on a box in the marketplace with whip marks on my back and terror in my heart,' he said. 'I had been taken away from everything and everyone I knew. I was so hungry that my body had begun to eat itself. The man who owned me had been unable to sell me time after time, and I knew that death was close.'

Lucius had been to the marketplace enough times to be able to picture the scene. There were always a few scrawny slaves that no one wanted.

'A man came out of the crowd and spoke to me,' Rufus went on. 'I didn't understand his words, but I heard kindness in his voice. He bought me and gave me food and clothing. He educated me and gave me work. He gave me dignity. I think you can understand what that must have been like.'

Lucius thought of the mockery he had seen in the eyes of Crassus and some of the gladiators. He nodded.

'That man was your father, and I have served him every day since then,' said Rufus. 'He is the best of men, and I will follow him and serve him as long as I draw breath. He had great power and now he has nothing. He has no money and no reputation. But he is my master. So yes, boy, he trusts me. Do you still doubt it?'

Lucius's head ached. All his ideas and assumptions were doing somersaults in his mind. He put his fingertips to his temples and rubbed them hard.

'Even if I accept what you say, I still don't understand what you are doing here,' he said. 'You've been here for weeks – why are you only speaking to me now?'

'I moved freely in and out of the city, even after your father left,' said Rufus. 'He wanted to know that his family was safe. He heard about Quintus taking the blood oath, and about your work here. So he sent me to watch over you both.'

Lucius felt a twisting pain in his chest. All this time he could have had word of his father. All this time.

'Why didn't you tell us?' It came out like a wail.

'I saw at once that Quintus is very angry with your father,' the gladiator said. 'I listened and watched, and I saw that he would not listen. If your father had attempted to communicate with him, he would have reported it.'

'No!' Lucius cried.

'Yes, I tell you. I know how to read people. But you… you were not so easy to understand. Your father believed that you could be trusted, but I had to be sure.'

'*Carpe diem*,' Lucius murmured.

'It was obscure,' Rufus explained. 'It told you nothing, but it was in your father's handwriting. I waited to see if you would tell your brother or your uncle, but you kept it to yourself.' A sudden smile flashed across his face. '*Almost* to yourself. I know you trust the little Egyptian girl.'

'Isidora wouldn't tell a soul,' Lucius said quickly. 'She's my friend.'

'Yes,' said Rufus. 'I think you have chosen well.'

'But why did he arrange to meet me and then not turn up?' Lucius asked. 'You know that he wasn't in the clearing last night?'

Rufus nodded. 'It was another test,' he said. 'We had to be sure that you could be trusted not to report him. I followed you to the meeting place – I made sure you hadn't arranged for soldiers to lie in wait for him.'

Lucius swelled with the unfairness of it. 'I have *never* believed that he was the Spectre!' he yelled. 'Everyone else thinks he's a traitor and only I stood up for him, and *I'm* the one you test? I *know* he's innocent!'

Rufus put one finger to his lips and nodded.

'My master knows where proof of his innocence may be,' he said in a low voice. 'As a slave-gladiator I cannot get to it, and he cannot risk returning to Rome. You are his only hope. He wants you to find it for him.'

'I knew it!' Lucius said eagerly. 'Tell me what to do!' He wanted to start at once, but Rufus shook his head.

'Your father will do that himself,' he said. 'I will take you to him tonight.'

'But you can't leave the school!' Lucius exclaimed.

'I will not be returning here,' said Rufus. 'I have done what was asked of me. From now on, it will be up to you.'

There was a shout from the arena – the gladiators were almost ready to depart for the amphitheatre.

'I must go,' said Rufus, rising to his feet.

'Wait!' said Lucius, putting his hand on Rufus's arm. 'Why fight, Rufus? You could take me to my father now!'

'If I disappeared now, just before my match, Crassus and your uncle would send men to bring me back,' said Rufus. 'Everyone would be looking for me, and we wouldn't get far. But later this afternoon, after my fight, no one will be interested in what I'm doing – they will be watching the rest of the gladiators. That is the best time for us to leave. We won't be missed.'

'But what if you get hurt and can't take me?' Lucius persisted, still holding his arm. 'Or what if you win – people will be hanging around you like flies.'

'You don't understand,' said Rufus, looking uneasy. 'I know that it will be all right.'

'You can't know that,' said Lucius. 'No one can look into the future; I don't care what the seers say. I only believe in facts and plain truth.'

'Then believe this,' said Rufus quickly. 'I am going to lose the battle today, but my life will be spared. As the loser, I will be unimportant and ignored, and we will be able to slip away without anyone noticing.'

'What are you talking about?'

'Your uncle and Crassus have an arrangement,' said Rufus. 'Some of the battles are decided in advance. Crassus gave me my instructions this morning – I must lose this match and I will be privately rewarded.'

He moved towards the doorway and Lucius could not hold him back.

'I don't understand,' Lucius said, still trying to stop him. 'Why would they do something like that?'

'Why do you think?' asked Rufus, looking back over his shoulder. 'Don't you have the measure of your uncle yet?'

'Money…' said Lucius, remembering the figures on the wax tablet he had found.

Rufus just gave him a look, and then he had gone. Lucius stood staring after him, hardly knowing what he was feeling. But something was flickering in his chest, like a little flame licking at dry sticks. He would see his father tonight! It didn't matter what Ravilla was doing, or whether Quin was skilled enough to fight tomorrow. Lucius would find the proof of Aquila's innocence, and Quin's match would be cancelled, and they would buy back their villa and life would return to normal.

Everything was going to be all right.

CHAPTER XIII

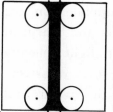t was the fly that brought Lucius to his senses again.

He didn't know how long he had been standing in the middle of the dormitory. His whole body felt heavy and immovable. It was as if someone had cast a spell and turned him into a statue. He felt the fly land on his cheek, but couldn't seem to raise his hand to brush it away. It crawled onto his nose, and he felt himself go cross-eyed as he tried to look at it. He laughed, and the spell was broken.

Still laughing, he opened his clenched palm and looked at the ring. It was shining like a promise. He slipped it onto his forefinger; it was only a little bit loose. Then he picked up the twisted twig broom and began sweeping the floor, gathering up the dirt with the cleaning sawdust. Tonight! He would breathe the same air as his father; he would learn why he had done such a desperate thing as to run away.

When the floor was clean and he'd scooped all the dirt and sawdust into the bucket, Lucius left the dormitory and walked out into the covered walkway. The arena was empty – even the gladiators who weren't fighting that day must have gone to see the spectacle. Lucius put down the bucket and broom, and walked out into the middle of the arena.

The midday sun beat down on his head and made him screw up his eyes into narrow slits. He tried to imagine how it must feel to face an opponent in this heat. It was hard enough to stand here and bear it in just his tunic. But the gladiators had to fight in heavy armour, and some of their weapons were excessively heavy. Lucius had felt the weight of the swords and shields in the armoury, and he couldn't even lift some of them. He would not last five minutes in a battle.

'Don't let Secundus see you daydreaming,' called Isidora's voice. 'He'll have you scrubbing the fountains if he thinks you like the sun that much.'

Lucius whirled around, trying to see her. The light was so bright that everything around the edge of the arena was a blur of shadow.

'I'm over here,' she said, laughing and picking up his broom and bucket. 'Did you leave these for someone to trip over?'

'Isidora, I've got amazing news!' he said, hurrying over to her.

He was so eager to tell her everything that the words spilled out of his mouth, tumbling over each other. She frowned, struggling to follow the chain of events.

'Wait, wait!' she said, holding up a hand. 'Come into the armoury – we'll be out of sight there.'

They dashed into the cool, half-empty armoury, and Lucius sat down on a bench and leaned back, feeling like an emperor.

'Start again, from the beginning,' Isidora said, standing in front of him with her arms folded across her chest. 'And for goodness' sake don't talk so fast. You found another message?'

'It was in my bag, just like the first one,' he said. 'It was definitely my father's handwriting, and it said to meet him last night and to tell no one.'

'And it was put into your bag *inside* the school?' she asked. 'It *must* be one of the slaves.'

'Stop interrupting,' Lucius replied. 'I'll explain everything. I went to the meeting place but there was no one there – I waited around for ages. I didn't know what to think – I was going to talk to you about it as soon as I got a chance today. But everything was so busy this morning, getting ready for the spectacle. And then Secundus sent me to clean the dormitories.'

Isidora gave a little start, but said nothing.

163

'Then Rufus came in. At first I thought he was going to attack me, but he showed me this.'

He held out his forefinger. Isidora stared down at the ring, and then looked back up at him.

'I don't understand.'

'This ring belongs to my father,' he told her. 'Rufus is his slave. He sent him here to watch over me and Quin, and to find out if we believed the stories about him being a traitor.'

She was not looking as excited as he had hoped.

'Lucius, this sounds really far-fetched,' she said. 'Why would your father make his slave become a gladiator? Why not just send him to see you at home?'

'Because Quin is never there,' Lucius snapped at her, annoyed that she was questioning him. 'He needed to know if he could trust us – me. There's proof of his innocence and he's going to tell me where to find it.'

'Just slow down a second—'

'Isidora, trust me!' he shouted. 'I *know* this is true!'

'And last week you *knew* Rufus was not to be trusted.'

'Look, I didn't believe it either at first,' Lucius said, reminding himself that he had been just as suspicious. 'But the place where Father asked to meet me was somewhere no one else would have known about. I mean, no one else would have known it was a place we explored together.'

'So why didn't he meet you, if you're so sure it was him?'

'Because it was a test,' he explained. 'They had to be certain that I wasn't going to turn up with a horde of soldiers to arrest him.'

'So now they trust you?'

'Exactly!' he said with triumph. 'After his battle, Rufus is going to take me to my father, and I'm going to find out where this proof is, and then everything is going to go back to how it was, and Quin won't have to fight tomorrow.'

Isidora frowned. 'But where *is* your father? What if Rufus gets hurt in the battle and can't take you?'

'That's another thing,' said Lucius. 'You know that wax tablet we found in the room underground? I don't understand it, but Rufus says that the money is something to do with the matches. Ravilla and Crassus are fixing the outcomes – they know who's going to win before the battle has even begun.'

Isidora had gone very pale. 'But that's wrong,' she said. 'It must be illegal – completely illegal.'

'When Father's back he'll sort the whole thing out,' said Lucius, glad that he didn't have to worry about it any more.

But Isidora's eyes seemed to be getting bigger and bigger.

'Lucius, where were you when Rufus was telling you all this?' she asked. 'Quick!'

'I told you – I was in the dormitory.'

'When – how long ago?'

'Half an hour – an hour – I don't know.' The urgency in her voice was making him feel uneasy again. 'Why?'

'Just before the gladiators left for the amphitheatre?'

'I don't know – probably,' he said. 'Yes.'

'I'm an idiot!' Isidora groaned. 'Why didn't I tell you straight away?'

'Tell me what?'

'Lucius, I saw your uncle standing outside the dormitories for ages before the gladiators left,' she said. 'He looked as if he was listening to something. I thought that maybe he was checking that you were working – I didn't know he might be listening to something like this!'

'He knows that my father is somewhere close by,' Lucius groaned. 'He'll have Rufus arrested – what am I going to do?'

'It's ten times worse than that,' said Isidora. 'Don't you see? Rufus has given away his secret – he told you about the match fixing and now he's planning to escape. Ravilla won't let him go, and if I know him he'll want revenge.'

'He can't risk Rufus telling anyone else about it,' added Lucius.

'I'm getting a horrible feeling about this,' said Isidora, her voice wavering. 'There's something really wrong happening here.'

Lucius stood up so fast that he made her jump.

'Rufus needs to know that Ravilla heard our conversation,' he said. 'It might change his mind about losing. Ravilla's the sponsor – he makes the final decision – and if he really does want revenge on Rufus…'

'Lucius, what are you going to do?' she asked.

'Run!' he said.

Lucius sprinted out of the school, hearing the thump of Isidora's steps close behind him. They would both be in serious trouble for abandoning their duties, but he couldn't worry about that right now. The temporary amphitheatre was only five minutes away – two minutes if they ran fast.

'Move!' he yelled at the backs of people who hadn't heard his footsteps behind them.

Bags and baskets fell to the ground as he dodged past people in a wild, headlong rush. Angry voices called after him and he heard Isidora calling out apologies, but all he cared about was stopping Rufus from fighting.

Lucius reached the amphitheatre first and hurled himself through the first entrance he saw. Suddenly something hit his ankle and he found himself sprawling on the ground, spitting sawdust out of his mouth. A very solid-looking man was standing over him, tapping the foot that he had just used to trip Lucius up.

'Tickets,' he grunted, folding his arms. 'Ever heard of them?'

'We don't need tickets, we're with the school,' Lucius panted, pulling himself to his feet. Blood started to trickle down his leg – he must have landed on a stone. He heard the roar of the crowd inside the amphitheatre and felt sick with dread – had the fights begun?

'We?' repeated the man. 'Think you're twins, do you?'

At that moment Isidora caught up with him, wheezing and red in the face.

'Please let us in,' Lucius begged. 'We need to speak to one of the gladiators urgently.'

The man's chest swelled with importance. He pointed up to the archway above the entrance.

'See that?' he asked, pointing to the number that was painted there. 'Know what that is?'

'I just want to—'

'That number shows which seats this entrance leads to,' the man said. 'Seats that have been paid for. Seats that have tickets.'

'We're not going to sit in any of the cursed seats!' Lucius yelled. 'Do we look like we're here to enjoy ourselves?'

'Slaves can't use this entrance,' the man replied. 'Your entrance is round the side. And I don't appreciate being sworn at. I'm only doing my job.'

'Look, we just need to get to the corridors, or wherever the gladiators are dressing,' Isidora explained. 'Couldn't you just let us slip through?'

'Not through here,' said the man. 'More than my life's worth. Only citizens through this gate, that's my orders.'

'This is an emergency,' Lucius said through gritted teeth.

'I can't help that,' he replied. 'Not my problem.'

'Can't you make an exception, please?' begged Isidora.

The man's pink, shiny lower lip jutted out and he shook his head.

'If I made an exception for you, every slave in the city would think they could slip in this way,' he said. 'You'll have to be smarter than that to get past me!'

Letting out an explosive roar of frustration, Lucius pelted along the side of the amphitheatre, passing three more citizens' entrances until he saw Posca standing beside an unmarked entrance arch.

'Have they started?' he asked him as he shot past.

'Yes, of course,' he heard Posca exclaim in surprise. 'What's wrong?'

'Wait for me!' called Isidora.

Lucius sprinted along the entranceway, and the clamour of the crowd seemed to get ten times as loud. At the end of the entranceway his path was blocked. There were, of course, no underground areas here, so the corridor was packed with cages, technical equipment and armour. He could hear the clash of weapons but he couldn't see who was in the arena. Isidora slammed into his back.

'Who's fighting?' she yelled in his ear.

'Don't know,' he shouted back. 'Got to get around this cage!'

Whatever beast had been in the cage that morning, it had obviously met its end in the arena, because the door was swinging open. Lucius squeezed through the narrow gap between the cage and the stalls, then tripped over a shield and sprawled on the ground for the second time in five minutes. Behind him, Isidora groaned. He looked up and saw Rufus bringing his sword crashing down onto Pulcher's small shield. They were too late.

Lucius rose to his feet and darted forwards to enter the arena, but Isidora grabbed the back of his tunic. She dragged him back and held on to his arm so tightly that he felt her stubby nails digging into his skin.

'Let me go!' he yelled. 'I have to stop the match!'

'Lucius, there's nothing you can do,' she said, looking frightened. 'The attendants would grab you before you got anywhere near him.'

'But he's got to know!' The words seemed to tear at his throat. 'We've got to shout to him – tell him!'

'How will he hear us over that?' Isidora asked, waving her free arm towards the stalls that surrounded them.

The shouts and cheers were deafening. Rufus's name was being chanted from twenty different directions at once.

'And even if we did make him hear us,' she went on, 'distracting him like that would only give Pulcher the chance to kill him.'

His head was throbbing, and tears pricked his eyes. The fire that had burned inside him a moment before had gone, and his body ached. Isidora's hand wasn't restraining him any more – it was holding him up.

'There has to be something we can do,' he said. 'There *has* to be.'

He remembered the loyalty in Rufus's eyes when he had talked about Aquila, and his stomach knotted into a spasm. This man was the only other person who believed in his father.

'I have to stop this!' he rasped. 'My father would find a way!'

'Your father was a senator,' Isidora told him. 'You're a slave. No one will let you speak.'

Her voice sounded thick and strange. When Lucius looked up at her, he saw that she was crying – she was giving in. *I'm not going to just sit here crying*! he thought. A desperate idea flashed into his mind.

'I might be a slave, but Ravilla is still my uncle,' he said. 'If I can just get to him, I can tell him that I know everything – I can threaten to tell the whole city about his cheating.'

'Blackmail?' Isidora looked shocked.

'It's the only power I've got!' he yelled at her.

She stared at him and then shoved him towards the stalls.

'He's halfway around the arena,' she said, pointing into the distance at Ravilla's seat of honour. 'Run, Lucius!'

Lucius scrambled up the steps, tripping over legs and bags, hardly feeling the blows that landed on his back. He reached the first tier's walkway and stumbled along it as fast as he could, trying to keep one eye on the gladiators as he went. It looked as if he had a little time. Pulcher was a good match for Rufus. They were both tall, and they had the same animal-like litheness.

Pulcher was using his spear to keep his opponent at bay, trying to stop the angled sword from jabbing around his shield. As Rufus turned to avoid the spear, Pulcher charged at him and slammed his round shield into the Thracian's side. Rufus crashed to the ground and Pulcher drew his sword, holding it diagonally in front of him.

Lucius looked towards his uncle again to make sure that he was heading in the right direction. He didn't seem to be any closer at all. He clambered past a group of young men, who gave him a shove that knocked him down once more. His knees were smeared with blood.

Pulling himself up, he carried on and glanced down at the arena. Rufus was on his feet again, and charging at Pulcher before the Hoplomachus could raise his spear. Their shields clashed with a resounding smash that echoed above the shouts of the crowd. This time Pulcher was thrown backwards, sliding helplessly across the sand. Rufus thundered towards him, his sword thrusting downwards, but it met Pulcher's shield as he launched himself upwards.

'Just keep blocking, keep him away from you,' said Lucius under his breath, willing Rufus to somehow get the message.

He was getting nearer – he could see his uncle's face clearly now. Below, Rufus was parrying Pulcher's attacks, but he wasn't fighting with the skill that Lucius had seen in training. He knew that he had to lose. The crowd was on Pulcher's side – they could see that he was pouring passion and spirit into his battle. Lucius wondered if he had also been told that the match was fixed.

'Fighting by the book!' shouted one man as Lucius scrambled past. 'Get back to training school!'

'Shame!' yelled another.

Lucius reached the steps that would lead him up to the next tier, but his legs wouldn't obey his command to run. He had to clamber up on his hands and knees like a child, his back to the arena. He wondered if Isidora was watching him – he thought he could feel her gaze.

There was a deafening roar and the crowd around him rose to their feet, punching the air, whooping and cheering.

'No, no, no,' said Lucius, turning around in dread.

Rufus was face down at the far edge of the arena – Pulcher had obviously sent him flying and knocked him out. His sword and shield lay on the sand between them.

Pulcher marched across the arena to his opponent as the familiar chant rose around Lucius: 'Kill! Kill! Kill!' Rufus rose onto all fours, shaking his head. His left arm was shining red with blood. He looked up as Pulcher reached his side, and then put his left hand on the Hoplomachus's thigh. From where he was standing, halfway up the steps, Lucius could see the bloody handprint it made.

He was too far away from his uncle – even if he had screamed what he knew at the top of his voice, Ravilla wouldn't have heard a word.

'Kill! Kill! Kill!' chanted the crowd.

Lucius saw his uncle gaze around the arena at the sea of outstretched hands, which all had the thumbs pointing out to the side – the sign for death.

Ravilla stood up and the chanting diminished. The verdict was about to be made.

'Spare him,' Lucius whispered. 'Spare him. Keep your word.'

He wished he could see the expression in his uncle's eyes. Ravilla seemed to be enjoying the moment and drawing it out. The crowd was silent, apart from a few isolated shouts of 'Death!' and 'Kill him!' Just when Lucius thought he couldn't bear it any longer, Ravilla raised his arm and held out his hand… with his thumb jabbing out to the side like a curved blade. Death!

'No!' Lucius shouted.

But the crowd's mass bellow of triumph blanketed his voice. He ran down the steps, not caring if he fell, not knowing what he planned to do. But before Lucius had even reached the bottom, Pulcher had thrust his sword into Rufus's neck.

'I can't believe he did it,' said Lucius.

'Can't you?' asked Isidora. 'I can.'

They were sitting against the outside wall of the amphitheatre, staring straight ahead. Lucius felt numb with shock and exhaustion. He had stumbled out of the amphitheatre by the first exit he reached, and somehow Isidora had found him.

'We can't stay here,' she said. 'We have to go back to the school before we're missed.'

'What's the point?'

'Lucius?' She turned to look at him, but he didn't move his head. He understood now why his mother just sat on her couch, staring at nothing. If he kept very still and very quiet, perhaps the numbness would never go away, and he would never have to think about all the things that had just gone wrong.

'Lucius, please,' said Isidora shakily. 'You're scaring me.'

'Go, then, if you want to go,' he replied. 'I'm not stopping you.'

'I'm not leaving you here. You can't just let him win.'

'Why not?'

He was speaking in a monotone and he knew it sounded strange, but there was something effortless about it too. At this moment, he didn't have any more effort to give.

'Because if someone doesn't do something to stop him, he'll just go on and on ruining lives,' she said with venom.

'Why bother?'

He half-hoped that she would give him a strong, solid answer, but none came. Her silence lasted so unusually long that he moved his head to look at her. She had turned her face away.

'Isidora?' he said to the glossy back of her head.

'There were so many secrets in his household that I lost track of what I was supposed to know and what I was supposed to forget,' she said. 'I heard my parents talking about one of the visitors who came to the villa in the middle of the night, and they mentioned a name.'

She drew a deep breath and her shoulders shook a little.

'I was just a stupid child,' she said. 'I didn't know what I was doing. I mentioned the name in front of him, and he questioned me. I told him that I had heard my parents say it.'

Lucius didn't know what to say, but something told him to reach out his hand. She took it in hers and squeezed it hard.

'Have you ever seen a slave scourged?' she asked. 'I don't suppose you have. It doesn't sound as if your father would use punishments like that.'

'No,' said Lucius, feeling sick.

'They use a whip with metal pieces tied to the ends,' she said. 'The metal rips the slave's back to the bone. He had them both scourged first.'

Lucius shuddered and she squeezed his hand more tightly.

'Then he had them crucified,' she said. 'It took my mother three days to die. My father lasted even longer.'

'Isidora…'

'I never even got to say goodbye.' She was trying so hard not to sob that the bones in his hand were half crushed. 'He locked me up until they were dead and thrown away like rubbish. Then he had me brought to him, and he told me what he had done. He warned me to remember what happens to slaves who betray their masters. Then he told me that he was going to show me mercy. He refused to have me in his villa any more, but he sent me to work in the school.'

Horrified, Lucius held her hand in silence. There was nothing to say. He had heard stories of people mistreating their slaves, of course, and he had agreed with his father that masters should treat their slaves well. But now that he and Isidora were friends, he knew that he had never truly thought of slaves as real people before. The way Isidora felt about her parents' deaths wasn't somehow less painful because she was a slave. It was no different from how he would feel if his parents were destroyed in such a monstrous way.

He watched her struggling to get control over herself. Her shoulders shook and her hand still squeezed his, but when she turned to face him she had dry eyes.

'I decided that I would never show him how he had made me feel,' she said. 'But that if I ever got the chance to take revenge on him, I would. Well, I think that perhaps this might be that time. So please don't ask me "What's the point?" All right?'

Without letting go of her hand, Lucius stood up and looked down at her. The numbness had gone, and he was ready to do something. It felt better than giving in.

'Come on,' he said. 'Let's go back to the school. I need to look inside Rufus's bag before the other gladiators come back.'

In the dormitory, Lucius and Isidora tipped Rufus's bag upside down. There wasn't much inside.

'A key, a tunic and a pair of sandals,' said Isidora. 'It could be the key to where your father is staying.'

'That's not much use without the address,' Lucius replied.

He placed the key inside the sandals and put them carefully back into the bag. Then he folded the tunic as neatly as he could. It seemed like the least he could do, but as he was folding it, he felt something hard.

'There's something inside the tunic,' he exclaimed, shaking it out. A wax tablet fell to the ground. For a moment, Lucius just stared down at it. It was more than he had dared to hope he would find. But would it tell him where his father was hiding?

He picked up the tablet.

My dear Lucius,

If you are reading this, you will already know that Rufus is your loyal friend. I am sorry that you have been kept in the dark for so long. There seems to be so much evidence against me that I did not dare to assume that you would not believe it. I hope that you can find it in your heart to forgive me.

There is so much that I want to say to you, but that can wait until we are face to face again. With your help, I am confident that we can find the proof of my innocence.

Rufus will bring you to meet me tonight, and I will explain the little plan that we have devised.

The hours will go slowly until this evening.

Quintus Valerius Aquila

Lucius felt as if he had walked into a stone wall.

'Nothing,' he said, passing the tablet to Isidora. 'No meeting place, no address, not even a hint of where he might be.'

'It's so clear that he's innocent,' said Isidora, reading the message. 'Why don't you show it to your brother? Surely he'll listen now?'

'Isidora, if I showed this to Quin he would take it straight to Ravilla. And I'm not sure that Father would want that to happen. After all, he isn't writing to *him*, is he? And Rufus as good as warned me against him.'

'What are you going to do?' Isidora asked, handing the tablet back to him. 'Don't forget, Ravilla must have overheard your conversation, so he knows that Rufus told you about the match fixing. You could be in danger yourself. You know he's coming back here after the spectacle tonight? I heard him say so.'

Lucius gritted his teeth. It was so unfair. Somewhere outside this vast city, his father was waiting for him. Somewhere there was proof of his innocence. Suddenly he realised something.

'If he overheard that conversation, he also knows that Rufus worked for my father,' he said, astonished that he hadn't thought of it before. 'He knowingly put his brother's slave to death!'

'And he knows that your father is nearby,' Isidora added. 'I thought that he was trying to find his brother, not keep you away from him.'

'*Why* did he do it?' Lucius asked. 'Why order the death of such a skilled gladiator?'

'Like Rufus told you,' said Isidora, 'there's bound to be money in it somewhere.'

The whole situation seemed more complicated by the minute. Lucius felt muddle-headed and confused.

'The thing is, I don't really have many choices,' he said eventually. 'It's no use going to Quin. I have no idea how to make contact with my father, and I can't tell the authorities, or Mother, or anyone that I would normally trust.'

'So what are you going to do?'

'I'm going to ask for an explanation,' said Lucius simply. 'I'm going to talk to my uncle.'

PART THREE

VETERANUS

CHAPTER XIV

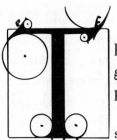he mess hall was ready, the barley gruel and boiled sheep's head were prepared and the slaves were waiting.

The sky was getting darker by the second – surely the spectacle would have finished by now? Surely the gladiators must be on their way back with Crassus and Ravilla?

But still the sky darkened, and still they didn't come. It was all very well boldly deciding to confront his uncle in the heat of the moment, but the waiting around was making Lucius's courage go distinctly off the boil.

Besides, he kept thinking about his father and imagining him waiting eagerly for Rufus and Lucius to arrive. He would wait… and wait… and wait… and no one would come. It was a miserable thought.

Eventually he went into a room beside Ravilla's study. Isidora had once shown him a crack in the wall through which conversations could be heard. He thought about the day she had taken him to the public bath-house to listen to Crassus and his uncle talking. That was the first time he had realised how well Ravilla could lie.

Lucius walked around the room and then pressed his hand against the wall it shared with the study. The darkness deepened, and the room around him faded into shadow, but he felt downwards until he came to the tiny crack.

He suddenly became aware of laughter and loud voices. The gladiators were returning, and in that instant Lucius knew exactly what he was going to do. He lay down flat beside the wall and pressed his ear against it. The voices of the gladiators grew muffled as they went into the mess hall, and then he heard someone entering the room next door.

'A success,' Ravilla said. 'And tomorrow will be even better – the Emperor will be there. And he's recalled all the patricians from their summer homes and country estates.'

'A success?' Crassus repeated, his deep voice vibrating in the wall. 'I lost the best fighter I've had in years – and I lost my bet. What's successful about that? I hope you know you'll be paying for it.'

'Stop bleating,' said Ravilla. 'You won every other bet we agreed. You haven't made a loss.'

'You owe me and you know it.'

There was a long silence, broken only by an occasional chink. It sounded like coins dropping onto coins. Eventually Crassus spoke again, sounding much more friendly.

'So are you going to tell me *why*?'

'Too much curiosity can be a dangerous thing,' said Ravilla.

Things were beginning to fall into place at last. Crassus and his uncle were somehow managing to place bets on their own gladiators, and then they were ordering them whether to win or lose. The gladiators had to obey – their blood oath demanded absolute obedience.

The next silence was so long that Lucius thought Crassus must have left the room. But then he heard the glug of wine, and realised that they were celebrating. He thought of Rufus's body being dragged away to the spoliarium* and wished that he had the strength – not to mention the bravery – to march into the next room and punch his uncle's sly face.

'Are you still sure about the lists for tomorrow?' Crassus asked. 'I'm talking about—'

'I know who you mean, and nothing has changed,' barked Ravilla. 'Not so many, of course – we don't want the Emperor to complain that our men are fighting by the book. But enough to make a little profit.'

* *spoliarium: the room where dead fighters were stripped of their armour.*

'He's got a lot of potential,' said Crassus. 'I didn't mind so much when I thought we'd still have Rufus. But now… he could be a real crowd-pleaser, you know. Good-looking lad. His mother won't thank you.'

'My sister-in-law is slowly but surely losing her grip on sanity,' Ravilla sneered. 'She probably won't even notice he's gone.'

Lucius felt as if something cold was trickling around his innards. Surely he must have misheard?

'We'll make it a good one at least,' said Crassus. 'Lots of flair and content – lots of style.'

'Plan whatever you like,' Ravilla replied. 'As long as Quintus is on his knees at the end of it all.'

Lucius clamped his hand over his own mouth, not trusting himself to be silent. His eyes stared blindly into the darkness as he wondered if his ears had deceived him. Could Ravilla really be sitting on the other side of the wall, calmly plotting Quin's death?

He heard Crassus say goodnight, and he rolled sideways until he could see out through the doorway. He watched the Doctor Retiariorum cross the arena and climb the steps to his quarters. Ravilla was alone.

Lucius stood up and made himself walk to the door. If he didn't do this now, he never would. He counted the steps to the door of Ravilla's study and paused in the entrance.

His uncle didn't see him at first. He was leaning back in his chair, his eyes closed. There was a cup of wine in his hand and a small lucerna on the table.

Lucius wondered if it was the one he and Isidora had used underground.

He kept still, and at length Ravilla opened his eyes. He jumped so violently when he saw Lucius that some of the wine sloshed onto the table.

'I didn't think you'd still be here,' he said. 'You startled me.'

Lucius didn't know what to say to this, and Ravilla's eyes flicked rapidly from side to side.

'Did you want something?'

With a flash of insight for which he thanked the gods, Lucius realised that Ravilla was afraid of him – afraid of the knowledge he might possess. He decided to reveal only what he had to.

'I know your secret,' he said.

Ravilla went scarlet. He stammered: 'I'm not sure I understand your meaning, Lucius.'

'I think you do.'

They stared at each other, and then Ravilla seemed to relax slightly. He waved his hand towards a chair.

'Please, take a seat.'

'I'd rather stand up.'

He had meant to sound grown-up, but it came out sounding petulant. A little smile played around Ravilla's mouth and he put down his wine.

'As you prefer,' he said. 'Now, you think that you know some sort of secret, is that it?'

Lucius stepped into the room on impulse, and then wished he hadn't. He glanced around at the door.

'There's no one listening, if that's what you're worried about,' said Ravilla, curling his lip.

'You'd know all about that, wouldn't you?' said Lucius, unable to help himself. Of course, that gave the game away. Ravilla's smile grew wolfish.

'Ah, I see. Rufus. Well, well.'

He pressed the tips of his fingers together and gazed up at Lucius.

'What exactly do you think you know, nephew?'

'You've been making illegal bets,' said Lucius. 'You've been fixing the games so that you win.'

Ravilla's fingertips parted again and he spread his hands outwards in a gesture of honest astonishment.

'A harmless deceit,' he said. 'Believe me, everyone cheats in one way or another.'

'No they don't,' retorted Lucius. 'And there's nothing harmless about it. Rufus wasn't supposed to die today, and I heard you just now, planning Quin's death.'

'A little joke between Crassus and me,' Ravilla said, picking up his wine and taking a sip. 'Of course Quin will not die tomorrow.'

'I'm going to tell the whole city about what you're doing here!' Lucius yelled.

'Oh, I don't think that's a very good idea, Lucius.' Ravilla's voice was so soft that Lucius had to strain to hear him. 'You see, I am only in this position because of your father.'

'My father would never tell you to cheat,' Lucius snapped.

'No, no, my dear brother was above anything so *earthy*,' said Ravilla. 'His crimes were far more intellectual. But when he needed to leave the city, who did he come running to for help? Mmm?'

'Are you saying you helped him escape?' Lucius asked in bewilderment.

'My dear boy, I spent every spare penny I had on getting your father safely out of this city and looking after you and your family,' said Ravilla. 'That's why I have had to be, shall we say, "creative" about finding new sources of income.'

'If that's true, then why didn't Rufus mention it?' Lucius demanded.

'Ah yes, Rufus,' said Ravilla. 'I wondered when we'd get around to him.'

He drew in a long breath through his nose, which flared white at the nostrils.

'Yes, I heard what he said to you this morning,' he went on. 'I was worried that you were being deceived, so, concerned for your safety, I eavesdropped. And, as I suspected, he told you a pack of lies. Aquila isn't anywhere near Rome. He is far away somewhere by now, wallowing in regret for his actions.'

'But—'

'Rufus was trying to trick you,' Ravilla said. 'It was a nasty, vindictive slave's trick, that's all. *I* got your father out of Rome. If you want to report me for that, go ahead. I'll be arrested, of course, and I will probably have to sell my property. I expect you'll be able to live here at the school, but your mother and Valeria may not be so lucky…'

Lucius was revolted. He stepped forward, placed his hands on the table and leaned in close to his uncle's smirking face.

'I don't believe a single word,' he said. 'I'm going to tell everyone the truth about you, including Quin. I don't care what oaths he made. He's not going to fight to earn you money!'

Even this didn't wipe the smug look from Ravilla's face.

'Lucius, I strongly advise you to learn the rules of a game before you begin to play,' he said. 'Quin signed his blood oath to the school – not to me. If he refuses to fight for any reason, he has already agreed to endure "branding, chains, flogging or death by the sword". The same will be true even if you have reported my little offence.'

Lucius sank into the chair. His uncle was right – he could do nothing to release Quin from his oath.

'However…' Ravilla went on.

Lucius looked up. His uncle's eyes were as sharp as knives, and he chose his words with great care, sounding some of them out slowly as if they were ripe fruits bursting in his mouth.

'Although it is not possible to remove Quin from the battle order altogether,' he said, 'I *may* be able to persuade Crassus to let him fight without a pre-planned outcome.' He let the words hang in the air before continuing. 'Of course, I would need to have *time* and *attention* to devote to such a difficult conversation. It would be impossible if I were *distracted*, for example, by worries about *legal* issues.'

It was blackmail, pure and simple. But Lucius understood that he was being offered his brother's life. He couldn't refuse.

'Do we have an understanding?' Ravilla asked.

Lucius swallowed hard. He had to keep his nerve.

'If you promise me that you will stop fixing the matches – *completely* stop,' he said, 'I will not say anything about what you and Crassus have done in the past.'

Ravilla pushed back his chair, stood up and gave Lucius a long, long look. Then he held out his hand. Lucius did the same, gripping his forearm. The touch of Ravilla's fingers on his own arm made his skin crawl. But Ravilla was smiling again.

'It is agreed,' he said.

END OF BOOK I

FOLLOW LUCIUS'S FURTHER ADVENTURES IN:

GLADIATOR SCHOOL II

BLOOD AND FIRE

ames given by Gaius Valerius Ravilla,' Lucius read aloud. 'Forty gladiators will fight. Perfumed water will be scattered.' His finger hovered over his brother's name. 'Quintus, Retiarius, tiro, will battle Burbo, Secutor. Has won ten bouts.'

'You've read it at least twenty times,' said Isidora, sounding rather impatient. 'You can't change the words by staring at them, you know.'

Lucius dropped the programme back into his bag and rubbed his eyes. He hadn't had much sleep.

'He should be battling another tiro, not a veteranus with ten palms,' he said.

'It shows how talented he is, that they've matched him with someone like that,' Isidora said. 'Thanks to you he has a good chance – now you have to leave the rest up to him.'

Lucius knew that she was right, but it was easier said than done.

They had squeezed themselves into the hot corridor among the cages again, this time with permission to watch a couple of matches before going back to the school. It was obvious from the arena floor that there had already been several gory fights, and the crowd's lust for death was growing. The air was rank with sweat and blood.

Lucius looked across the amphitheatre at the Emperor Titus, who was leaning back and laughing with Ravilla. He wondered if Titus knew that one of the gladiators he was about to watch was the sponsor's nephew.

Quin and his opponent, Burbo, were already in the arena doing their warm-up exercises. Burbo had a few supporters calling his name, but the crowd loved an underdog and there were just as many people shouting Quin's name and wishing him luck.

There was a hush as the musicians signalled the start of the battle, and then a sense of anticipation as Quin circled around the heavily armoured Secutor, feinting with his net. Burbo raised his sword and Quin jabbed at his leg with the trident. Burbo deflected it with his shield and sprang towards Quin, who darted backwards. There was a roar of approval from the crowd – it was a good start.

Circling again, Quin shook his net playfully across the sand, taunting his opponent. Burbo charged at him but he sprang aside, casting the net as he leapt. The Secutor avoided the net and charged at Quin again, but Quin could run faster than anyone Lucius knew.

He breathed a sigh of temporary relief as the heavily armoured Secutor chased his brother around the arena. Burbo had no chance of catching him. Quin's advantage was speed and lightness – Burbo would tire out far more quickly.

After several minutes, Quin drew nearer to Burbo again, staying at trident's length. He started to circle him faster and faster, making Burbo turn on the spot to keep him in sight.

'He's trying to make him dizzy,' said Lucius, clenching his fists. 'Come on, Quin, faster!'

As if they had heard him, the crowd took up the chant – 'Faster! Faster!'

Quin threw his net and lunged with his trident at the same time. But Burbo's experience showed and he avoided them both, slashing at Quin's back with his gladius. Quin arched quickly away from him, but not quite quickly enough. The gladius drew a long, shallow cut across his back and bright-red blood trickled down. The crowd howled in delight.

'First blood to Burbo!' they yelled. 'Come on, Burbo!'

Lucius could tell from the way his brother's chin jerked upwards that Quin was annoyed to have been the first to be cut.

'Keep your temper,' he muttered under his breath. 'Stay focused.'

Quin slammed his trident into Burbo's leg so fast and hard that the Secutor went down with an almighty crash. The crowd erupted, but Burbo was on his feet again in an instant – the greave on his leg had protected him.

He stamped on the net that was lying on the sand and slashed at it with his gladius. Quin jerked the net from under Burbo's foot and sent him crashing to the ground, but he rolled sideways and scrambled to his feet again, hurling himself after Quin.

The battle ranged across the full breadth of the arena, giving everyone a chance to see the gladiators up close. When they neared the corridor where Lucius was squatting, he saw that they were both sweating and bleeding freely, but neither of them had a serious wound. This could take a long time. Lucius felt as if the inside of his skin was turning cold, despite the stifling heat.

Quin led Burbo back into the centre of the arena, every now and then flinging his net without letting it go, forcing the Secutor to jump over it like a child's skipping rope. The crowd screamed with mocking laughter.

'Dance, chaser, dance!' they shouted.

Burbo was getting tired. The weight of his armour was gradually making him slower, and the crowd shouted louder still, sensing weakness.

'You've got him now, Quin!'

'Don't let him rest!'

'Make him chase you again!'

'Charge him!'

They were so loud that their shouts of advice to the fighting men reverberated inside Lucius's head. Burbo seemed to have heard them too, because he suddenly charged, his gladius up, and knocked Quin's trident from his hand. Burbo gave it a kick that sent it flying across the arena. Quin turned to run after it, but before he could get away, Burbo grabbed him by the tunic and hauled him backwards. Lucius cried out as the blade of the gladius flashed down, but Quin was ready. He threw his net over Burbo's head and gave a powerful tug on the mesh. Burbo stumbled and crashed to the sand.

Quin released his net as Burbo lumbered to his feet, and then flicked it towards Burbo's legs again. This time the Secutor's jump was too slow. The net whipped around his legs, throwing him down once more.

Faster than thought, Quin rushed forward, picked up his trident and used it to knock the sword out of Burbo's hand. Burbo lunged after it, but his legs were still enmeshed. Quin stood over him, pointing the prongs of his trident at Burbo's throat.

Burbo's chest was heaving as he gasped for air and raised the index finger of his left hand.

'He's asking for mercy!' Lucius cried.

'He's won!' shouted Isidora, jumping to her feet. 'Yes!'

Quin released Burbo from the net and the young Secutor knelt at his feet.

'Kill him!' shrieked the crowd. 'Kill him!'

'Spare him,' said Lucius, staring at his brother.

Isidora put her hand on his shoulder.

'It's the Emperor's decision today,' she said.

Please don't make him kill, Lucius thought. *Don't make him do that. Not today.*

Titus was quick to give his verdict. He stood up and held out his palm with the thumb covered. Lucius's bones seemed to turn to jelly.

'Mercy,' said Isidora. 'He must have thought that they both fought well.'

'Thank the gods,' said Lucius.

He looked at his uncle, whom he could just glimpse behind Titus's throne. Did Ravilla know that he was somewhere in the crowd, watching him? Lucius hoped so. He had a sudden surge of wellbeing and self-belief. Anything seemed possible.

'He's got away with it this time, but I know him now,' he said. 'I know what he is. Truth's a powerful thing. One day I'm going to expose him for the cheat he is. But first I've got to find Father and clear his name.'

Isidora didn't reply. She seemed to be deep in thought. Quin was jogging around the arena with his first victory palm, waving to the crowd. They were screaming his name, and he looked reinvigorated. Titus was standing up, holding a metal plate that contained a pile of coins.

'Lucius, let's go,' said Isidora, tugging on his tunic.

'In a minute,' he replied. 'I want to see Quin get his prize.'

'No, listen, I've been thinking,' she said.

'It can wait for one minute!'

'Remember the wax tablet you found in the underground office?' she went on as if he hadn't spoken. 'It didn't make any sense because we didn't know what it was about, but we do now. I think we should go back down there and take it!'

'We can't just take it!' said Lucius.

'Why not?' she demanded. 'Weren't you just saying that you want to expose him as a cheat? This could be the proof you need.'

'I didn't think you were actually *listening*,' said Lucius, grinning at her despite himself. 'Besides, I gave him my word not to say anything about the match fixing as long as he stopped it straight away.'

'Oh, yes, because you can always trust Ravilla to keep his promises,' said Isidora.

She had a point. Twenty minutes later, Lucius was inside the underground office, with Isidora urging him to hurry up.

The leather boxes were still empty apart from the wax tablet. He took it and stuffed it into his messenger bag, wishing that he didn't feel so guilty.

'It's like being at war,' he told himself aloud. 'Sometimes you have to do things you're not very proud of.'

'What did you say?' hissed Isidora from outside.

'Nothing.'

'What's taking you so long?' she asked, poking her head around the door. 'I don't like it down here.'

'It was your idea,' he said, stepping around the desk and picking up the lucerna.

'Stop!' she exclaimed. 'What's that?'

She pointed at the floor beside the desk. Lucius peered down.

'I can't see anything.'

'I'm sure there was something – it must have been the way you were holding the light. Bring it lower.'

They crouched down and Isidora gave a cry of triumph and picked up a small roll of thin lead.

'What is it?' she asked.

Lucius took it and peered at it. It was dirty and had obviously been there for some time. It was pure luck that she had seen the light fall on a small, unmarked piece of metal.

'It's a curse tablet,' he said. 'My uncle must have dropped it without realising.'

'We have those in Egypt too,' Isidora commented. 'What does it say?'

'I'm not going to read it, Isidora!'

'Well I will, then,' she said, taking it back from him. 'I'm not scared of your gods.'

She carefully unrolled the soft tablet and held it close to the lamp while she read the words aloud.

'To you, ferryman and death-bringer Charon, I invoke by your name in order that you help to hold back Aquila, to whom my mother gave birth, and turn his life to wretched darkness, shame and torment. Make him suffer and remove him from my presence, and let him meet his end in a bad way. Quickly, quickly!'

'Let me see that!' said Lucius, snatching it from her.

He read the text through three times, his thoughts whirling. Then he looked up. The flickering light was making their shadows jump on the walls.

'Have the gods helped to shame my father?' he asked. 'How can I fight against their magic?'

'Shake yourself out of it, Lucius,' said Isidora in her most sensible voice. 'There's nothing divine about what happened to your father.'

Lucius pushed past her and blundered back along the dark passageway. He didn't stop until he reached the top of the steps and could stand in the bright sunlight again.

He took several deep breaths. There was something very unpleasant about that underground room. It made him feel panicky. Even now, the damp mustiness of it seemed to be clinging to him.

He walked across to the fountain and drank. Then he splashed water onto his face and combed it into his hair with his fingers. Isidora followed him and placed her hand on his arm.

'I'm sorry,' she said. 'Did I offend you?'

'No,' said Lucius. 'I just couldn't stay down there and think straight, that's all.'

'So you don't think that this was the "will of the gods"?' she asked, holding out the little lead tablet.

'No,' he said, taking it from her and looking down at it. 'All this curse proves is that my uncle wanted to get rid of my father. Maybe he managed it.'

'What do you mean?' she asked.

He looked up at her and felt a surge of hope.

'Don't you see?' he asked. 'Ravilla told me that he helped Father to get away, but what if he was the one who denounced him in the first place?'

'Ravilla's capable of anything, I know that,' said Isidora. 'But I don't understand why you're looking so pleased about it.'

'Because if Ravilla was behind the denouncement, I think there's a good chance that he has the proof my father was looking for,' Lucius explained. 'Rufus said that I was the only one who could get it, and I didn't understand what he meant. But that would make sense if it's hidden in Ravilla's villa or something. I'm his family – I could get access. If I could find the proof it might not matter that I don't know where Father is.'

'That's a lot of ifs,' Isidora pointed out.

Lucius knew that she was right. Finding the proof his father needed was not going to be an easy task. But he had just watched his brother defeat a fully armed Secutor gladiator while wearing little more than a loincloth. Today, anything seemed possible.

After the musty darkness of the underground office, the warmth of the sun seemed to give him strength. It was as if the gods were telling him that he had the power to turn his fortunes around.

'Ravilla's behind what's happened to us, I know it,' he said. 'And somewhere there is bound to be evidence of what he's done.'

Isidora stared at him, and then gave a little nod. Lucius knew that she would do all she could to help. He filled two of the fountain cups and handed one to her. Then he raised the other.

'Here's to friendship,' he said.

'To friendship,' she replied.

He lifted his chin and straightened his back. Strength and certainty were surging through him. One day he would prove his father's innocence. In the meantime, he had a friend who he could trust with his life. He had a brother who was the hero of the gladiator school. These were riches – greater riches than he had ever understood before.

Whatever the future held, Lucius was ready to face it.

TO BE CONTINUED…

FIGHTERS IN THE

Hoplomachus, 'the Hoplite
 (Greek infantry) fighter'
Weapons: spear, gladius, dagger
Shield: small, round, usually bronze
Helmet: Greek style, with crest
Armour: arm guard, thigh guard
Opponent: Murmillo or Thraex

Murmillo, 'the Fish Man'
Weapon: gladius
Shield: large, oval or rectangular
Helmet: enclosed, with fin-shaped crest
Armour: arm guard, greave
Opponent: Thraex or Provocator

GLADIATORIAL ARENA

Retiarius, 'the Net Man'
Weapons: trident, net, dagger
Shield: none
Helmet: none
Armour: arm guard, galerus
   (shoulder guard)
Opponent: Secutor

Thraex, 'the Thracian'
Weapon: Thracian dagger
Shield: small, rectangular, curved like
   part of a cylinder
Helmet: wide-brimmed, often decorated
   with a griffin
Armour: arm guard, thigh guard, greaves
Opponent: Murmillo or Hoplomachus

A selected list of Scribo titles

The prices shown below are correct at the time of going to press. However, The Salariya Book Company reserves the right to show new retail prices on covers, which may differ from those previously advertised.

All Scribo and Salariya Book Company titles can be ordered from your local bookshop. Visit our website at:

www.salariya.com

They are also available by post from:

The Salariya Book Co. Ltd,
25 Marlborough Place
Brighton BN1 1UB

Postage and packing **free** in the United Kingdom

GLADIATOR SCHOOL
BOOK 1

BLOOD OATH

HOPLOMACHUS
'the Hoplite
(Greek infantry) fighter'

Weapons: **spear, gladius, dagger**
Shield: **small, round, usually bronze**
Helmet: **Greek style, with crest.**
Armour: **arm guard, thigh guard**
Opponent: **Murmillo or Thraex**

www.scribobooks.com/gladiatorschool
© MMXIII The Salariya Book Company Ltd

GLADIATOR SCHOOL
BOOK 1

BLOOD OATH

MURMILLO
'the Fish Man'

Weapon: **gladius**
Shield: **large, oval or rectangular**
Helmet: **enclosed, with fin-shaped crest.**
Armour: **arm guard, greave**
Opponent: **Thraex or Provocator**

www.scribobooks.com/gladiatorschool
© MMXIII The Salariya Book Company Ltd

GLADIATOR SCHOOL
BOOK I

BLOOD OATH

GLADIATOR SCHOOL
BOOK I

BLOOD OATH

RETIARIUS
'the Net Man'

Weapons: **trident, net, dagger**
Shield: **none**
Helmet: **none**
Armour: **arm guard, galerus (shoulder guard)**
Opponent: **Secutor**

www.scribobooks.com/gladiatorschool
© MMXIII The Salariya Book Company Ltd

THRAEX
'the Thracian'

Weapon: **Thracian dagger**
Shield: **small, rectangular, curved like part of a cylinder**
Helmet: **wide-brimmed, often decorated with a griffin**
Armour: **arm guard, thigh guard, greaves**
Opponent: **Murmillo or Hoplomachus**

www.scribobooks.com/gladiatorschool
© MMXIII The Salariya Book Company Ltd